THE MYSTERY OF THE
PILGRIM TRADING POST

YOUNG AMERICA BOOK CLUB

A Division of Weekly Reader Children's Book Club

Presents

The Mystery of
THE PILGRIM TRADING POST

by *Anne Molloy*

Illustrated by Floyd James Torbert

HASTINGS HOUSE, PUBLISHERS

New York

Published simultaneously in Canada
by S. J. Reginald Saunders, Publishers, Toronto 2B.

Library of Congress Catalog Card Number: 64-13478
Printed in the United States of America

CHAPTER ONE

UNWILLING VISITORS

"Come on, you young ones, hop aboard. We'll do our getting acquainted on the way home," Cousin Mary Peter Tibbetts called from the driver's seat of her old car.

Two boys and a girl had just filed down from the high, aluminum-sided bus at the filling-station stop. They were the only passengers for this town far down the Maine coast; the rest would go on to the next stop across the Canadian border. Now, stiff from hours of riding and somewhat bewildered in the bright sunshine, they walked toward their cousin's car.

The new arrivals from Boston were thirteen-year-old twins, Will and Lettie Dennis, and their cousin, Jonas Wingate. Although the twins had looked forward to meeting Jonas this morning, they had disliked him from the first. And they felt from the tone of his few words on the trip that, although they were cousins and of the same age, he disliked *them*.

Cousin Mary Peter beckoned them on gently. Her car

doors were waiting open like the spread wings of a bird.

"Come on, stow your gear in back there; plenty of room, especially for such small bags. They don't look half big enough for folks that have come to stay all summer," she said. Her voice was a bit gruff but her blue eyes were kind.

Will and Lettie exchanged glances that meant, doesn't she know we came for a week's trial, that we don't have to stay if we can't stand the place? As for Jonas's feelings about this visit, they couldn't read his face. So far it had worn but one expression, that of scorn for everything they had seen together from the crooked streets of Boston to the Maine countryside.

"Sit any way you want," Cousin Mary Peter invited, "but be sure to slam the doors hard. They jiggle open in nothing flat on these rough roads."

Will climbed into the front seat by Cousin Mary Peter. He knew without looking that Lettie was scowling at being in the back with Jonas. The car doors banged. Then, with a roar and a lurch, the car shot out into the main street. The town was so small that they were soon among open fields. They were green and rolling, returning to the wilderness for the most part, and sprinkled with daisies, buttercups, and the red-orange of Indian paintbrush. Beyond were the peaked tops of evergreens that continued on and on as far as the eye could see. It was hard not to believe that they didn't stretch straight to the Arctic Circle.

"Why would anyone want to shoot for the moon when they can come here? It's just as lonesome." Although Jonas spoke low so his older cousin wouldn't hear, his tone was scornful.

"Sorry to drag you off before you could even get a look at the town, but the bus was quite late and I've got folks waiting back home and along the way, too, for prescriptions," Cousin Mary Peter explained. "I'm sure you've

8

been told that I'm the village druggist and sometimes what amounts to the doctor. There's none for miles."

"I know, I know, Mother told me," said Jonas impatiently.

"That so?" said Cousin Mary Peter. "And what else, I

wonder? That I live alone in my haunted house and keep rather strange hours. That I eat when it suits me and work in my store?"

"Well, as a matter of fact," Lettie admitted tactfully, "Mother did say you didn't exactly live by the clock."

"That's right," Cousin Mary Peter continued. "Too many rules and regulations when I was growing up, I guess. I had too much living on the dot. These days I cook one big meal and sort of scrabble for the rest. Hope you won't mind. Talking of food reminds me I'm hungry. Will, if you are Will, reach in the glove compartment and find a bar of chocolate. It's in there somewhere. Divide it in four and pass out the pieces, will you? Also, hand me a little brown bottle that's in there. I promised Lucy Hibbs I'd leave it for her. Yes, that's the one."

Suddenly she applied the brakes. Her passengers all jerked forward as the car halted before a dreary gray house.

"I won't be more than a sec," said Cousin Mary Peter. Bottle in hand, she strode toward the house.

"You wouldn't think anyone could live in such a ramshackle place," said Jonas. "The whole thing tips back, house, ell, barn, and all, as if any day they'd go toppling over like a line of domino soldiers."

This was the most human remark her cousin had made so Lettie agreed with him. "I don't think I'm going to like it here the least bit," she said. "For summertime, it's cold and gloomy. And what will we do all day? Cousin Mary Peter isn't going to help us pass the time, is she?"

"Say," Jonas burst out, "did you two want to come in the first place? I sure didn't. My Dad and I had camping plans all made, the trip to the Rockies we've always talked about. Then when this invitation to Surprise Harbor came, plans got changed. My mother said one of us ought to be here for one last summer in the old Tibbetts homestead. I'm it, worse luck."

Now his cousins could understand Jonas's scornful attitude.

"We didn't much want to come, but we didn't have much to leave. Our dad was signed up to teach summer school and we'd have stayed right home," said Lettie.

"Speak for yourself," said her brother. "Maybe you didn't have plans. I did. This was the summer I was going to get rich, mow lawns and all, and in between times work hard on tennis. I wasn't the least bit crazy about coming away."

"It was our mother that was crazy about our coming. She acted as if it were the end of the world when she got Cousin Mary Peter's letter saying this was the old house's very last summer." Lettie smiled at her cousin.

"My mother was the same way. You'd think the Tibbetts homestead was the first, best, and most beautiful house in the whole country." Jonas looked more agreeable every minute.

"What do you think, Jonas, should we tell our cousin we're sorry her house is being torn down so that a new bridge can be built? Maybe she'd rather not talk about it," said Lettie.

"Golly Moses, call me 'Jo!' Nobody uses my whole name. Maybe that's one thing I've got against the Tibbetts house, my being named Jonas for the one who built it," said Jonas.

"Jo it will be," said Lettie.

Cousin Mary Peter's return ended the conference.

"If ever there was a more contrary lot of coots than the people 'round here, I'd hate to see them," she began as they drove off. "They claim they've got to have your medicine. You turn yourself inside out to get it to them. Then

11

they tell you they've sent off for some packaged poison they've read about and then have the gall to blame you because *your* medicine doesn't seem to be helping them. It's frustrating and no mistake. Now, where's my choc?"

"Oh," said Will, embarrassed, "I forgot. We got talking."

He divided the candy bar which he had been holding. Cousin Mary Peter popped a square of chocolate into her mouth and the others were quiet as they ate.

Then Will asked their cousin the question they had discussed. "How much longer are the bridge people going to let you keep your house?"

"Just as long as I can stave them off. The day they come to start tearing it down they'll have to drag me out of it kicking and biting, I can tell you." She accelerated the old car to prove that she meant this.

Even so a large black car overtook and passed them. The rush of its passing shook the smaller car. The blast of its horn made them all jump.

Cousin Mary Peter shook her fist at the disappearing rear end. "That's the villain himself, that Bart Simes. He's the one who had the bridge idea in the first place. Wangled poor old Ebbie Thaxter's half of Eden Island away from him and now he wants the government to build him a bridge out to it so's he can make lots of money from it. Talks of making Smuggler's Cove out there into a lobster pound, having a marina to attract the yachting trade, and dear knows what all. He doesn't care who gets trampled on. Tear down a fine house, ruin the loveliest island there is, it's all the same to Bart."

"But how can just one man get a bridge like that?" asked Will.

"Huh, by pretending there's others that want it, that's how. Bart got lots of the folks about, mostly the ones that

12

owe him money, to sign a paper asking for the bridge." In her bitterness, Cousin Mary Peter accelerated even more. The red speedometer needle vibrated angrily as it moved higher.

"I've always known Bart," their cousin continued. "It seems we've been natural enemies from the first. In school he was top boy and I was top girl, and, if I do say so myself, sometimes I was top, period. We were always pitted against each other in everything from catching the biggest haddock to rowing the fastest to Eden Island. Now with this bridge ruckus I don't speak to him if I can help it. Funny part of it is, he still phones over for medicine when he has the least little stomach-ache. Probably because I cost him less than a doctor."

"Couldn't you poison him?" asked Will with a croak so doleful that they all laughed.

"Now you're talking," said Cousin Mary Peter. In her glee she drove even faster. "That's just what I'll do—put a bit of arsenic in his next prescription."

They rattled on over the rough roads. Suddenly the driver applied the brakes so abruptly that Will's forehead bumped the windshield. "Drat it! Whoa, whoa," she said as they stopped before a weathered shack. "I almost forgot, the Vances' youngest is teething and kicking up. Will, dig me out that white bottle from the compartment."

He found the bottle under a pile of candy wrappers. She hurried into the little house with the medicine.

"I hope she's got something to mend a broken head," he said, rubbing his bump.

"For a snapped neck, too," said Lettie. She rotated her head to discover whether she still could. "Cousin Mary Peter is—well—sort of unusual, isn't she?"

"Plain crazy is what my dad thinks," said Jo, "to bury herself down here. He says she has all kinds of ability. But then he did have his heart set on that camping trip, so he wouldn't approve of her now."

Their cousin ran back to the car and on they swept.

The last few miles were traveled almost in silence. The passengers felt obliged to watch the road ahead as their cousin's driving became more dashing. She swept around blind corners and tore up hills so sharp that chimneys appeared long before the houses beneath them. Except that politeness kept them from shrieking, it was like being on a roller coaster.

At long last Cousin Mary Peter said importantly, "At the top of the next rise you can look down and behold the ancestral mansion."

She shot them up over the next crest and leaned forward in anticipation.

"Drat," said Cousin Mary Peter. "Fog's rolling in just the way it generally does when you want to impress strangers. Oh, drat."

A swirling white mass like heavy smoke was swallowing houses and barns and dark, pointed spruce trees.

"If you look quick, you can see our chimneys," she said, but even as she spoke the red bricks were drowned in a white tide of fog.

"Too bad," said Lettie, because someone should.

The advancing fog engulfed them, too, and soon their view was limited to the edges of the road. Will turned to the back seat. For the first time the exchange of glances between the arriving cousins was three-way. They were in silent agreement to dislike this place. Cousin Mary Peter didn't seem to know that they had come for a week's trial; they must tell her tomorrow.

Today they wondered if they could endure a week in the old Tibbetts place.

CHAPTER TWO

THE "DOWN-WITH-BLACK-BART SOCIETY"

Somehow they couldn't tell Cousin Mary Pete the next morning that they were to stay only a week.

For one thing, she talked eagerly of what they would do in the long summer ahead.

For another, the loveliness of the day made it hard to talk of leaving. The fog had swirled off to its home in the east and the world, so damp and dismal last night, was now bright and beautiful. The old Tibbetts homestead, they found, faced both sun and sea. Beyond it the harbor and bay sparkled blue with golden flecks. Inside the old house ceilings rippled with golden reflected light. A fresh breeze blew curtains back into the rooms and brought in a constant clamor of gulls and the *slap-slap* of waves against ledges.

Furthermore, the first smell of cooking bacon that twisted up the steep back stairs was so delicious that they forgot their resolve.

"How will you have your eggs?" was Cousin Mary Peter's morning greeting as they trooped into the kitchen. "Since this is your first day, I stayed home to get your breakfast. That way I can show you the ropes. From tomorrow on you scrabble for breakfast yourselves. I've got Ebbie Thaxter in my shop to stave off customers."

She waved them to places at the oilcloth-covered table. "After we eat I'll give you the Tibbetts homestead Grand Tour, from top to bottom. On second thought, though, I'll leave the attic for you to explore come foul weather, as it's bound to. Now tell me, is sunnyside-up okay for your eggs?"

"Sunnyside-up," was the cheerful chorus. It described more than the way they wanted their eggs: it showed their feelings about the day and the place.

In the middle of breakfast the back door opened. A grizzled, weather-beaten face under a wide-brimmed felt hat peered in. "Mary Pete," the man asked, his jaws working as if he chewed a cud, "you want to come over to the shop a minute? Bart, he's phoned up—"

"Drat, Ebbie, didn't I tell you to take any messages that come?" Cousin Mary Peter rattled the stove lid and jabbed at the kitchen fire.

"Ayuh, so you did. But I'm more'n likely to get 'em all bolloxed up. Don't want to be guilty o'causing you to poison your customers, do I? Bart, he did say suthing 'bout some more o' that stomach sarse you fix him."

"Oh, dear, wouldn't I like to sarse *him*," she answered. "He's been off banqueting with some of his politician friends at the state capitol, I'll be bound, trying to get them to back his everlasting bridge. He's got himself a good case of indigestion in the process, I'll warrant. Run back, Ebbie. Tell him I'll get at the prescription for him just as soon as I can. And, oh, yes, this is Dora's boy and girl here, and this is Delia's boy."

"Ayuh, thought so." Without a change of expression, Ebbie studied them. When he shut the door behind him they knew they were memorized.

Their cousin sighed. "Whew, try and get that one to take any responsibility. Well, I can count on him to let Bart know who my visitors are. Incidentally, why don't you just call me Mary Pete, the way everyone does? All this 'Cousin Mary Peter' business makes me want to look around to see who on earth you're talking to. I was supposed to be a boy named Peter. When I came a girl, my folks stuck on the Mary. Now, if you've had enough breakfast, we'll do that Grand Tour."

They followed her through the house into the front hallway. Mary Pete opened the wide front door. A soft wind scented with wild roses, rockweed, and spruce needles swept in.

From the center of the hall a staircase as graceful as a harp and as delicate went up to the second story. Halfway up it divided at a landing, then continued up on two sides to become an upstairs hall. The mahogany handrail was dark but all the rest of the woodwork was painted white. It was carved with airy patterns, and scrolls, rosettes, and leaves stood out like frosting on a wedding cake.

"Every bit of this carving was done by hand and with no tool but a jackknife. Our ancestor, the first Jonas in the country, kidnaped the man who did the work in Dublin, Ireland. We don't know how or why, simply that he got him aboard his vessel, and once here, kept him at it till the very last rosette was done."

"Oh, but it is beautiful!" Lettie tipped back her head to follow the tracery of scrolls up the side of the stairs.

"Isn't it?" Mary Pete agreed. "All this new part, as we call the front of the house, has the finest woodwork you can imagine." Her voice took on a careful dignity that was very different from her usual everyday speech as she described the house. Although she had grown up with its grandeur, the old house still affected her.

"How old is this new part?" asked Jo.

"Couple of centuries, built just after the Revolution. The old ell where your rooms are was once the main house. That goes back to dear knows when. The very first house was a log cabin on the spot. We have always firmly believed that it was the very place where the Pilgrims set up a post to trade with the Indians when they came from Plymouth to this bay of ours. If only we have something definite to prove it, I doubt if Bart or anyone else could tear this place down. Then it would be a national shrine and tourists would come for miles to see the historic spot."

"Do you suppose it's too late to find some evidence that the Pilgrims did come here?" asked Jo eagerly.

"Maybe we could. Oh, we've got to save this beautiful place!" cried Lettie, forgetting all yesterday's dark thoughts about it.

"Why don't we try?" said Jo.

From that moment, without words or a meeting, a society was formed. It began with their exchange of resolute glances.

The Grand Tour continued. Now they had a purpose beyond simple admiration. They looked in each room for a place where evidence of those newly-important Pilgrims might be found. They looked into wide cracks for hidden documents, they touched bits of carving that might hide the spring of a secret drawer or hidey hole. As they moved from sun-flooded parlor to library to upstairs chambers, Lettie always exclaimed, "Oh, this room is even more my favorite!" and the boys wasted not a moment in the search for hiding places.

Finally Mary Pete laughed at their eagerness. "Oh, don't think I haven't been looking ever since the time I was knee high to a grasshopper. I've always been fascinated by the thought that the Pilgrims and the Indians met here to do trading. Wanting some evidence of it to save the house is just a new version of my old kid excitement. Oh me, oh my, how certain we've always been that this was the bartering spot, but to try and prove it is another thing. Of course, we do have proof positive that the Indians used to come here in great numbers. They left their shell heaps behind them to show that they feasted here on clams and oysters."

"Where are these Indian shell heaps, where?" asked Jo. "Indians are what I go for. Dad and I were going to do some digging on that trip of ours—"

"I'm surprised that your mother never told you about the shell heaps. I guess in the summers she came here she was more interested in hemlines and hair-dos than in Indians," said Mary Pete.

"Tell us where the shell heaps are," begged Jo.

Mary Pete screwed up one eye and looked mysterious. "Might be more fun if you discovered them yourself, don't you think?"

"I guess so," Jo answered reluctantly, "but I want to get right at it."

"As for me, I must get at that prescription of Bart's. After all, I do run a business. But I may put that bit of poison in his order just the same. If you want to keep on exploring, you'll find the boathouse key hanging under the kitchen shelf. I'll be right there in the shop next door if you want me. Help yourself to eatables when you're hungry and tonight we'll boil some lobsters for supper."

She was gone before they could answer.

"We were going to tell her first thing about our not staying for more than a week," said Will.

"We were going to ask which room was the haunted one," said Lettie.

"Let's not tell her about leaving until suppertime," Jo

suggested. "Golly Moses, whatever shall we do first now? Hunting for those Indian shell heaps is my first choice."

"Exploring the boathouse is mine," said Will.

"Looking over the attic would be mine, but I suppose Mary Pete is right; we ought to leave that for bad weather," said Lettie.

"Sure," said Will. "Let's go to the boathouse. That's quicker than hunting for shell heaps."

To his surprise, the others agreed on that. They hurried back to the kitchen and from under the shelf took the key tagged *Boathouse*. As they ran with it toward the shore, they saw a large black car whirl past the house on its way to the harbor. Lettie shook her fist at the somber vehicle.

"There he goes, the cause of all this trouble. Maybe we ought to start a club and call it the 'Down-with-Black-Bart-Society.'"

"That's a good hating sort of name," said Jo. He repeated it as they ran.

Will, in the lead, called back over his shoulder, "Could be in our week here we can do something to stop his old bridge."

Then they gave in to the pleasure of running pell-mell down the steep slope. The long, feathery grasses, starred with daisies, brushed softly against their bare knees. Ahead lay the boathouse to explore, and, who knew, in it might be the clue they needed to save the old house.

CHAPTER THREE

THEY DISCOVER A WHIRLPOOL

The boathouse padlock was rusty and reluctant to open but finally Will, perhaps because he was the most eager to get inside, was able to turn the key in it. Together he and Jo swung the two wide doors apart.

Lettie, peering over their shoulders, exclaimed, "Whew, I can't see much but cobwebs and rust."

Her brother saw other things. "Boats!" he cried. "Look at 'em. I never saw so many kinds all at once!" All thoughts of Black Bart left him. His sole desire was to launch a boat and as quickly as possible. "Grand Banks dories stacked up, a peapod, skiffs, a sailing dinghy," he recited.

Ever since he was old enough to read he had studied books on boats in the public library. Now here at hand were many of the types he had known only at secondhand. He looked and looked, and was too excited to say more.

Jo and Lettie studied the heaps of fishing and marine gear. Rusty anchors, dip nets, seine nets, barrels of red wooden lobster buoys, and one of glass ball floats.

At the very back of the building, in front of a pair of doors, Will discovered a dory small enough for them to move out. He shot the rusty bolt holding the doors and pushed it open.

In rushed the wind and out swept angry swallows which had been scolding and chittering at the newcomers from their mud-pocket nests.

"Come on, Let, just don't stand there dreaming," her brother ordered. "Pick out a pair of oars that are the right size and then help us shove out this dory, will you?"

Lettie answered doubtfully, "Do you think we should? Mary Pete didn't say we could."

"Why else would she tell us where the key was if she didn't intend us to use her boats? This isn't a museum. We can both row and swim."

"Me, too," said Jo.

"What are we waiting for then? Let's get going." Already Will was straining to move the dory. Jo tugged on the opposite side and Lettie, still a bit uncertain, pushed from the stern.

It took a great deal of pushing to get the boat outside but once they had it on the ways sloping down to the water, Will was exuberant. "From here on the going's easy. It'll be a cinch."

They all ran at the dory and gave a shove that should have been powerful enough to carry it to the water. It moved only a short distance; it took a great deal more shoving and pushing before the stubborn orange bow hit the surface of the harbor. Then Will leaped aboard and capered a moment in his joy. "Come on, you fellows, climb aboard!" he ordered. "Jo, into the bow, Let, the stern."

"Look who's captain," was her retort, but she didn't really mind being bossed today. It was fine to be on the bright water. "Isn't Mary Pete's house just beautiful from here? It's so white and sort of smiling with the sun on its face. And there's a widow's walk on top. I bet we could see all the way to Canada if we went up there."

"Where we bound for, Captain?" asked Jo. "Are we going to roll, roll down to Rio?"

"Tomorrow we will," answered his cousin. "Today we'll investigate something near. See those white birds that aren't terns nor gulls nor anything else I know?" Will jerked his head toward the bay where on its current-streaked surface there were scores of white birds. They hovered in a ragged garland or whirled about like weather vanes.

"Yes," said Lettie, "there's millions."

"Well, we're going over and study them and discover what they are. I thought we'd be farther on our way there than this. Even with these long oars a dory is harder to row than I thought. I wish we had another pair so two could row."

Will rowed for a time in silence then he added, "And I wish you two would get lower down; it would help. You aren't exactly streamlined when you stick up so."

Obligingly his passengers plumped themselves down on the floor boards.

"O-oh, the boat's leaking. I've sat down in a lot of water," wailed Lettie, "cold water, too."

"Golly Moses, the water is coming in for sure. Look, Will, see these little waterfalls all along this one crack in the side," exclaimed Jo.

Will jerked his head to look, and somehow his abrupt movement released an oar. It slid out from between the two wooden thole pins that held it in place. He leaned out at once to retrieve it but his arm wasn't long enough. The dory was too high sided for him to reach that oar and cling to the other between its thole pins.

"Grab it, Jo, grab it before it gets past you!" Will shouted.

Jo leaned out over the water as far as he dared but the

oar slid past his outstretched fingers as if it had a mind of its own. On and on it sped, bobbing and turning upon itself, toward the whirling, darting sea birds.

Will groaned. "Why, oh, why can that oar travel so fast on its own and we can scarcely move? It's you lumps of passengers just sitting there, that's the trouble."

"What else can we do?" asked Lettie calmly. She was used to Will's angry spells and wanted to show Jo how to deal with them.

Will said nothing. He began to paddle furiously with the remaining oar. It thumped against the sides as he shifted it and picked up orange paint. Soon Lettie was complaining of being wet from the water he scooped onto her in the process of shifting. As for the runaway oar, it increased the distance between them all the time.

It's like the White Rabbit hurrying to an appointment, Lettie thought. She didn't say so; the scowling Will was in no mood for frivolity.

Finally Will said, "No soap. We aren't moving. I'm going to try skulling. That might work better than this paddling. Move your carcass, there, Lettie, and we'll switch places."

The exchange was made. Will laid the shaft of the oar in a semicircular notch that had been cut in the stern's narrow transom. Then he wiggled the oar blade back and forth in the water.

"Maybe this will work," Will said. "I've read about how you do it, but I've never tried it."

By this time the lost oar had completely disappeared and the dory was making little headway.

Suddenly Jo shouted from the bow, "Turn the boat around, Will! Turn it while you can! There's a whirlpool beyond us where all those birds are."

"Whirlpool?" asked Will.

24

"Yes, sir. I mean it. That's what made the oar skedaddle so fast. It got caught in the current and pulled along. Don't you see the whirlpool now?" Jo asked as he pointed.

All three stood cautiously to look across the water. Now the others could see the whirlpool, dark streaks of current winding into a common center. Here was a glassy funnel of sea water, a terrifying version of what happened in the bathtub when the plug was pulled and water rushed down the drain.

"Turn around, Will, turn the dory 'round!" Jo shouted.

Will returned to his skulling and tried to head the bow toward home. The only result was that the dory traveled sideways instead of bow first.

Lettie was down on the floor boards once more. As she shivered and crouched, she envied the strange sea birds. They could fly over this dangerous spot and leave it at will. She hugged her knees and tried not to think about a story she had once read of people sucked into a maelstrom of circling water.

"If only we had a bailing can we could at least get rid of some of the water in the dory," Jo said, although he knew they had none.

The whirlpool drew all their attention. They never thought of looking away from the vortex that was nearer all the time. So absorbed were they that a small boat with a powerful outboard motor surprised them as it planed up to them. It circled the dory and set it rocking in its wake.

"Why, it's Black Bart, I bet you anything," Lettie shouted.

"Sh-sh, he'll hear you," Will said. The boat was coming close.

It was Bart Simes, he said so himself, as he came alongside. Then he called, "Got a line aboard there, you kids? Throw it to me if you do and I'll tow you in."

Will longed to accept this offer but he answered, "Maybe we can make it by ourselves."

"Thank you all the same," said Lettie, making her voice as icy as her wet feet because she spoke to their common enemy.

"Don't be such goons. Of course you can't make it in. Been watching you for the last half-hour through my binoculars. I would have come sooner only I thought you needed a lesson. Now if you've got a line there, throw it. What about that line roved through your bow. Is that any better than a spiderweb?"

Jo picked up the bow line. It was weathered gray and very soft but he threw it toward Bart. It fell into the water far from the mark. Jo hauled it in, coiled it, and tried the shot again. Bart caught it. As he fastened it to a cleat in the stern of his boat, he fussed at the three in the dory.

"Mary Pete's a mighty smart woman. You'd think she might have been smart enough to warn you about taking out old boats that haven't been in the water going on a hundred years or so, especially dories. They're likely to drop their bottoms out. And she should have told you several other things, such as how strong the current sets off here. And how, when the tide comes piling in, you can expect the whirlpool."

"Mary Pete is a very busy woman," said Lettie in her icy tone.

"And I'm a busy man. Let's go," Bart almost growled.

He pulled the starter cord on his motor and they moved off in a great curve. The dory, heavy with water, yawed from side to side like an animal being led to slaughter. Lettie was the only one who looked back at the whirlpool. She wanted to gaze down into its glassy funnel but Bart had snatched them to safety too early. She could only study small whirlpools like dimples that dotted the surface around them.

From time to time Bart turned to check on his tow. Will, as captain in the dory, felt he must wave to show all was well. He did it in a moderate sort of way; they mustn't give Black Bart the false idea that they wanted to be friendly.

They were almost off the boathouse when the water in the dory stopped sloshing and the miniature waves corrugating its surface vanished. The old line had parted, they realized. Bart had left them behind. Soon he missed his tow and circled back.

"It's a miracle the bottom didn't drop out of that old-timer you picked to have yourself a time in. As I said, there's a whole lot Mary Pete ought to tell you. Too bad she's so busy," he called to them.

Lettie stood up for Mary Pete. "This morning," she said, "she had to hurry off and put up a prescription for someone foolish enough to get himself upset banqueting with politicians." Lettie hoped that she sounded both dignified and unfriendly.

"So that's what she told you," Bart said curtly with a dark scowl. "Well, I guess you don't need my help any longer. You're practically in now." His tone implied that it would do them good to struggle on with one oar. "For the love of Mike, if you kids have to get in scrapes, at least do it in a seaworthy boat. Come over any time and borrow one of mine. All Mary Pete's got need a heap done on them, caulking, painting, probably a whole lot more. Yes, you come over to my wharf. I'll fix you up with a boat."

Lettie was about to say, "No, thank you," in the icy tone she was beginning to enjoy, when Will spoke. "Thanks, we may do that."

Bart planed off toward his wharf.

"How could you say you'd borrow a thing from him?" said Lettie.

"Don't you see," said her brother, "it will give us an excuse to go over there. You never can tell, we might just discover he was up to some skulduggery. We could use it against him to save the old house. At least it would make it easier to keep a watch on him."

Jo agreed with Will. "Yes, it might help us if we could hurt him."

"Even if he did save our lives, I still hate him. Makes me think of a shark or something, the way he smiles," said Lettie. "Oh, Will, get a wiggle on and get us ashore. I'm just about frozen, sitting in all this ice water."

Although the old dory was logy with water, it was out of the strong current. Will skulled them to the boathouse. Here they found two rusty cans and bailed out the water. Even so, the dory was still heavy from what it had soaked up in its dry boards. They struggled and tugged to get it halfway up to the door.

"Oh, I'm too starved to tug a bit longer," complained Lettie. "Let's go get some lunch and come back and finish then."

The boys agreed to this.

"We'll tie her up so she won't drift off if the tide comes up," said Will.

"After that," said Jo firmly, "we hunt for shell heaps. I'm counting on them to turn us up something important, something important enough to end Bart's old bridge before it's even started."

CHAPTER FOUR

EARTH AND WATER

Scrabbling for a meal took longer than they expected. In the first place they spent quite a bit of time in finding the food. The old house had so many odd cupboards and pantries that they had to hunt for what they wanted. Then, when their hunger was satisfied, Lettie wasn't pleased with the appearance of the kitchen.

"What a mess!" she exclaimed, her nose wrinkled in disgust, "all these milky, sticky, eggy dishes. I'm going to wash them. It's the first time I ever wanted to do such a thing. Maybe it's because Mary Pete didn't ask us to."

Jo felt that washing the dishes might be a dangerous action. "She will expect you to the next time," he said.

"*You* don't have to. I'm going to," Lettie announced.

She turned to the dishes and to her surprise Will joined her. She took the humming teakettle from the stove and poured hot water into the dishpan. Will refilled the kettle. Water came in a great leap from the iron pump by the sink as he moved the handle up and down although it did protest, *oh, don't, oh, don't.*

Before Jo left the house, he told them what direction he planned to go. They followed his route when they had finished the dishes. It took them through a tightly packed line of spruce trees along the far side of Mary Pete's shop. Then they went over a tumbled stone wall. This brought them into an open field.

A flock of dipping, chattering goldfinch flew over. One Jersey cow with a mouthful of grass and daisies was the only occupant that they could see.

"Cow, Cow," Lettie called, because she suddenly felt gay from being in this airy, open place, "can you tell us where the Indians made their shell heaps?" Not a *moo* came in answer. Lettie whirled on one heel to enjoy the complete circle of sky.

"Let's go, Let," said her brother impatiently.

They ran down the sloping pasture, in and out among great scattered boulders, toward the shore. Suddenly from a far corner came a hail. Jo was standing on a mound and waving excitedly.

Will paused only long enough to make a trumpet of his hands and shout through them, "Coming!" Then he and Lettie ran.

When they reached Jo they found him bent almost double. He was probing the mound with a stick.

"What luck?" asked Lettie.

In his excitement Jo stuttered. "P-p-lenty," and straightened up. "This is one I'm on— an Indian shell heap, I mean!"

He waved the stick with which he had been digging among daisies and hawkweed. Will and Lettie climbed up beside him on the large ant heap of a mound. They peered into the hole. The exposed earth was very black and speckled quite evenly with bits of white broken shell.

"Jiminy!" said Will in an awed voice.

"Indians!" said Lettie in the same tone. After a pause she added, "Did they grind the shells all up like this?"

"Nope," said Jo, "don't imagine so. Probably they got that way from being here in all kinds of weather, you know, freezing and thawing and stuff, busted them up this way. Golly Moses, we ought to find most anything here—arrowheads, stone scrapers, fish weights!"

Once more he attacked the mound with his stick.

"I should think you'd get a shovel," said Lettie. "Why don't you go to the woodshed? There's all sorts of tools there."

"Okay," said Jo, and he was off, running as if he meant to return before they could discover something valuable.

That was just what the other two hoped to do. They poked and prodded and sifted by hand. But when they sighted Jo returning they had found nothing larger or more interesting than a bird bone.

Jo flung the spade he carried onto the ground and himself beside it. "Got a stitch in my side from running," he said with a groan. "You can use the shovel till it goes."

Feverishly they set to work. By the time Jo's stitch had gone they were knee deep in a crater and had found neither Indian nor Pilgrim leavings.

"How long would it take these Indians to eat all the clams or oysters or whatever was in the shells?" asked Lettie.

"Years and years, I guess," Jo answered. "They used to come every year to the same place. I've read all about it. They would eat some of the clams right there. The women would dry the rest in the sun or smoke them over a fire."

Jo joined them and, turn and turn about, they worked with the spade. They made a small mountain of freshly dug earth. But they found nothing.

Finally Lettie sat down to rest. "I'm so hot and tired and

thirsty that I could drink a well dry. Let's go to Mary Pete's drugstore and get a coke."

"Let's," said Jo, and drove the spade into the earth until it stood alone. "Whatever's here in the heap will wait for us that long, I guess." He led the race toward the drugstore.

Mary Pete's old shop was built in the manner of all such from Augusta to Abilene to Alaska. Its roof was flat and the false front hid it from the road. A huge mortar and pestle with only a trace of its original gilt stood at the peak. The faded sign over the door read, "Jonas Tibbets, Druggist." Sign and building were both a weathered gray. In fact, the only brightness on the outside was furnished by two teardrop glass globes that hung in the windows on either side of the door. One globe was filled with red liquid, the other blue. Their reflected colors stained the ledge beneath them red and blue.

The jingle of a bell hanging on the door told Mary Pete they had arrived. She parted a pair of curtains at the back of the shop and joined them.

"I'll warrant you've come to ask me a question," was her greeting. "I left in such a hurry that I forgot to tell you which room is the haunted one. Don't worry it's mine and I've never seen our ghost. Those that have report a lady with a red shawl over her head who climbs the front stairs laboriously at night and then opens a drawer in my bureau. I've never had the luck to meet her."

"Poor ghost," said Lettie with a delighted shiver, and her imagination went dancing off until she forgot why they were here.

Jo remembered. "That's not really what we came for," he told his cousin. "We wanted to tell you we'd found a shell heap and we've been digging in it so hard we've got to have a cold drink."

33

While he spoke his eyes, like those of the other two, studied the store. The soda fountain they expected was not here. Neither were there postcard racks, magazine stands, sunglasses, or bathing caps.

Mary Pete read their puzzled expressions. She laughed. "I can see you don't know what to make of my drugstore. That's what it is, a drugstore, pure and simple. Nary an ice-cream soda or candy bar in the place. But let's see now." She turned to the shelf behind her. "Yes, here they are. This is what passed for candy in the old days. I still carry them because I like them—colt's-foot rock and horehound drops. Help yourselves."

She set two glass jars down on the counter and took off their wide stoppers.

Horehound drops were the choice of all three, perhaps because they looked more like candy than the other. The fluted, pencil-thin sticks of colt's-foot rock were like pillars in a set of building blocks.

"H-m, good," said Lettie as she tasted the pleasant sweetness of her drop. "What lovely bottles you have all around your shop, Mary Pete."

"Come in the next bad day and really look them over. I'll give you a lesson in pharmacology to boot, if you'd like. But not right now; I'm working on a prescription for Hoyt Simpson's wife. Then I'm going to send Ebbie along with it. At the same time, he'll pick up the lobsters for our supper. That's what I do, take out in trade what Hoyt owes me." Then Mary Pete called into the back room, "Ebbie, is Hoyt's boat in yet?"

A creak and the sound of a vacated chair rocking itself to a standstill came from the back room. "Ayuh, he be. Leastways he's just coming in 'round the island," Ebbie answered.

"In that case, I'll hustle and get his prescription done

for him. Then you can skedaddle over there and bring back our lobsters. I'll warrant that by the time they're ready to eat these three young ones will have found something interesting in the Indian shell heap."

"Injuns," was Ebbie's scornful reply, but the word was all the cousins needed to make them want to resume their search.

Before Jo turned to go he said, "Maybe we ought to tell you what we did this morning, Mary Pete. We took one of your dories out of the boathouse and, well, we got ourselves adrift in her. That Bart Simes came out with his outboard and rescued us. He towed us in. I hope you don't mind our letting him."

"No. That was nice of Bart, I'm sure," said Mary Pete with mild sarcasm. Then she exploded in a great sigh. "Oh, dear, what kind of guardian am I? I should have warned you about taking out any of my boats; they haven't been in the water for a coon's age. Maybe Ebbie will help you make one of the skiffs good and watertight."

"Maybe." Ebbie shrugged. "All of them boats leak like sieves, them that don't leak like baskets, but if you say to fix up a skiff, Mary Pete, that's what I'll do."

The three cousins went off to quench their thirst at the kitchen pump.

"I'm glad you told Mary Pete about our rescue, Jo," said Lettie. "It was better for us to than for someone else."

"That's what I thought," Jo answered.

"Yes," Will agreed, "hearing it that way she might have ordered us to stay out of all boats. That would be no fun, even if we're just here for a week."

They returned to their digging. They widened the crater in the shell heap a great deal but they had nothing to show for their work except reddened palms and blisters from the spade.

"My back is broken. I'm hungry. I'm going to stop," said Lettie.

"Great whirling dervishes, you don't have to stay," Jo scolded. "I thought you wanted to help save the Tibbetts place by turning up some evidence of a Pilgrim trading post. Go, if you want to. I'm staying. Maybe I'll turn up something before supper. Go, but don't forget to call me when the lobsters are ready."

He attacked the shell heap with renewed energy. As Lettie crossed the pasture toward the house she was convinced that if the answer to the mystery of the Pilgrim trading post were there, Jo would find it. Either that or strike China with the spade.

CHAPTER FIVE

ANTIQUES AND HORRIBLES

Supper that evening was a lesson as well as a meal. The three cousins had never eaten boiled lobster from the shell; Mary Pete showed them how to extract the white flesh from the lobster's scarlet armor.

"Don't neglect the little legs," she said as she sucked on one; "some of the sweetest meat is in them. Now, tell me, Jo, how did your hunt in the shell heap go?"

"Didn't find a thing except broken pieces. But I'm going to, if it takes me a week." Jo had been about to say, "If it takes all my week here," but he couldn't. He tossed a red lobster leg into the large dish—Mary Pete called it "Mama's cream pan"—put in the center of the table for discarded lobster bits. Mary Pete was so gay, the room so cozy with the fire in the range, the lobster so good that Jo couldn't bring himself to say he was to leave at the end of the week. Nor could Will nor Lettie. They were under the same spell as Jo.

Mary Pete snapped off a large claw and said, "This afternoon I remembered our old copybook that was used for writing in cooking receipts. Some woman in the family, no one is sure who, wrote in it, 'My mother, aged ninety, says she can recall the days when the Injuns came here—sometimes a hundred canoes on the shore and over across on the island they have their campfires and hullabaloos.' No name, no date, but there it is, between a rule for roly-poly pudding and one for making dandelion wine."

"What in the world is a 'hullabaloo'?" asked Lettie.

"Your guess is as good as mine. What it sounds like, I imagine, a gathering that goes on and on with lots of singing and dancing. And, speaking of hullabaloos, tomorrow is the Fourth of July. It's been a long time since I took much part in the excitement but you three will want to. We always have a parade of Antiques and Horribles in Surprise. As for costumes, the attic is at your service," said Mary Pete.

The back screen door opened and in came Ebbie with an armload of firewood. He let it fall into the woodbox with a loud crash. When he had straightened up he announced, "Just seen Bart down to the wharf when I was getting the lobsters off Hoyt. Bart said to me, says he, 'Tell Mary Pete to keep an eye on them young ones. What's more, tell her I got a surprise for her on the holiday and one for the whole darn town.' "

"I don't know about the whole darn town," answered Mary Pete, "but I expect to be more surprised than pleased at any of Bart's doings."

Ebbie nodded. "I imagine," he said. "You want I should run you any more errands, Mary Pete? Fog's starting to come a-rolling in and I thought I'd like to row over early tonight and get to the island before it shuts in."

"No, guess not, thanks, Ebbie. See you in the morning," Mary Pete said.

38

Ebbie lunged off with his rubbery
bery cud.

"I thought you told us that Ebbie
island to Bart Simes for making a
said Jo.

"So he has, but he lets Ebbie
place. Every year the old buildin
bie uses less of it. Now he's sort of
kitchen. Bad winter weather he stays over here, sleep
couch in the room back of the shop. Bart makes a lot of
Ebbie, brings him little presents when he goes on a trip,
you know, stuff like hotel calendars and soap and all. Anyhow, Ebbie half thinks that Bart is pretty good." Mary Pete
had a faraway look on her face as she spoke.

"Where does this Bart live? Has he moved out to this
part of the island he bought?" asked Lettie.

"Mercy, no. He lives in a great ark of a place at the other
end of town. It sprouts turrets and bay windows wherever
his grandfather could possibly stick one to show the neighbors how rich he was. Old Mrs. Trafton, who is poison neat,
keeps house for Bart." Mary Pete stopped, sighed, and then
said briskly, "Let's talk about something that's fun. Let's go
back to the parade business. You all must march. It's been a
long time since anyone from this house did."

"I'm going to be a Horrible," said Will.

"Me, too, a horrible Horrible," said Jo.

"Not for me. I'm going to be an Antique. Maybe there's
a lovely old dress up there in the attic that would be just
right," said Lettie.

"Oodles, oodles. Help yourselves to anything up there."
Mary Pete paused. "Hark! I think I hear Old Growler, the
foghorn, blowing out there. Ebbie's fog is in. I should judge
he had just about time to make it across to the island be-

in thick. In all probability, with the wind sou'- will be in all day tomorrow. It'll be the right sort for attic rummaging."

As Mary Pete predicted, the fog was still in the next day. Windowpanes were milk glass and all sounds were softened by the white vapor. Even the mournful notes of the bell buoy not far offshore were swallowed in it.

Jo, Lettie, and Will hurried through breakfast to get to the attic as soon as possible. As Lettie laced her fried eggs with red ketchup lines, she reminded the boys, "We haven't said a word to Mary Pete about seven days' trial."

"I really forgot all about it," said Jo. "But we ought to tell her at supper tonight, shouldn't we?"

When their eggs were eaten, they started for the attic. At the foot of the stairs they hesitated a moment. Each was remembering that here was where the ghost climbed its toilsome way.

Jo said, "If you crash into a ghost on the stairs, are you supposed to say 'Excuse me'?"

The others laughed, but a bit nervously. The front hall in foggy weather was not the cheerful place of yesterday.

At the top of the second stairs, steep and straight, they stopped to accustom their eyes to the gloom. The great unfinished room was dim; its three windows almost obscured by fly-spangled cobwebs.

"Golly Moses, what fog," Jo said. He ran to the small high dormer at the back and stood on a chest beneath it to look out.

"You can't see a thing from here except the ell roof, the kitchen chimney, and that big old lilac bush by the kitchen door. Everything else is fog, fog," he reported.

"Never mind the old fog, Jo. Let's get busy on costumes right away, huh?" said Will.

40

Where to begin? They stood hands on hips and studied the wealth of treasures. It was an orderly confusion. Sea chests, packing boxes, trunks, cardboard boxes stood in rows under the eaves. Among them were discarded household articles . . . a cradle, spinning wheel, three-legged stool, and a dressmaker's dummy told homely bits of family history. Overhead in a space between two huge chimneys and just beyond the top of the stairs were bunches of dried herbs. They hung by strings from the rafters and, as a gentle breeze stirred the tags tied to them, they twirled like mobiles.

There was so much to discover that it was hard to remember why they were here. Will fell into a trance over a sea chest full of nautical instruments. Jo carried an old book under a window to read its title and, forgetful of all else, read on and on in the brown-edged pages. A stuffed owl invited Lettie to stroke its glossy head and stare back into its glassy eyes.

Finally Will made a decision about his costume.

"This feather duster settles it for me," he announced. "I'll be an Indian chief and paint my face until I'm a horrible Horrible. The duster will be my headdress."

A tin funnel decided Jo. He picked it up and put it on his head. The fit was so perfect that he knew at once what he was to be. " 'The Tin Woodman' from *The Wizard of Oz*, that's for me. I'll hunt up a lot of empty tin cans to cover my arms. Then I can slap some aluminum paint on cardboard for the rest of me, the part I can't cover with real tin. It'll be a cinch. Of course, I'll latch onto Ebbie's ax and carry that."

Lettie's choice was taking a long time because being an Antique was more serious than being a Horrible. She raised the lids of trunks and chests one after another. Carefully she lifted out all sorts of garments and returned them as

carefully to their tissue papers. She found a Civil War uni-
form with its red sash lying between newspapers, its dark
blue dotted with moth balls. She found dresses with tight
sleeves and some with ballooning sleeves. One was of em-
broidered lawn as delicate as gossamer and another was of

material that almost stood by itself. The boys were losing patience with her for not making a final selection.

"Oh, come on, Let, will you?" said Will. "I want to get out of here and start practicing on painting my face."

At once Lettie saw herself deserted and alone with the ghost in its red shawl toiling up and up toward the attic.

"Wait, Will, wait," she begged. "I wouldn't go off and leave *you*."

Will agreed to stay a bit longer. He occupied himself in making Indian faces before a cracked mirror.

Lettie's search was getting desperate now. Not one of the dresses was right. Then at the bottom of a great trunk she found one of gauzy pink with so strong a smell of camphor that she had to hold her breath.

Jo slammed shut the book he had returned to and called out, "Oh, hurry, Lettie, can't you?"

"If only this pink dress fits, I'll be done," she said. It was over her head and she was wriggling into it. "Help me, Will," she called to him, "help me. It doesn't want to slide over my blouse."

Will groaned but he tugged the long skirt down and helped fasten countless hooks at the back. The belt could only be hooked after a great pulling in of her waist. Then she moved toward the corner where the cracked mirror stood. The dress made a silken murmur as she walked. As she studied the dress and herself, she heard footsteps below in the front hall.

"If that's Mary Pete down there, call and ask her to come up, one of you. I want her to see this nice dress," she said.

Will obliged. He thudded down the steep stairs. At the bottom he called, "Mary Pete, come on up, please."

There was no answer, but somewhere in the house he heard a door shutting. He ran upstairs again and crossed the attic to the small dormer window at the back. If he could get it open he could call to Mary Pete from here and save time.

He jumped up onto a chest below the window and looked out.

Someone was leaving by the back door. A figure moved off into the fog. It wasn't Mary Pete, he was sure of that; it was a man.

"Hey," he reported to the others, "Mary Pete wasn't downstairs but a man was. He's just left."

"Probably Ebbie," said Lettie as she strutted a bit in the long pink skirt.

"Nope. It wasn't the right shape. He's so stooped over, I could tell him. I could swear it was Black Bart," Will said.

"What in the world would he of all people be doing in Mary Pete's house? I don't think she'd want him wandering around. Which way did he go? Toward the shop to see her?" asked Jo. He had joined Will on the chest beneath the window although he knew that nothing could be seen through the fog by this time.

"No, sir. The fellow disappeared in the direction of the village. I'm going to run down and follow him. If it's Black Bart, I want to find out what he's up to. Anyone that's acted the way he has ought not to come in here without being checked." Jo clapped the tin funnel on his head and ran down the stairs. Will followed.

"Wait, wait for me, please!" wailed Lettie. "I'm a prisoner in this dress. I can't unhook it by myself."

"Can't stop. Come with the dress on," were Will's last words before he disappeared.

Both boys knew that they must hurry to catch whoever left by Mary Pete's back door. Black Bart, if it were Bart, would soon be swallowed up in the fog. If he had taken something from the house, they must find him before he had a chance to hide it.

They had gone but a short way when Will suddenly seized his cousin's arm. "Stop and listen," he urged in a low voice. "I don't hear footsteps. Maybe the fellow dodged off to one side. Maybe Black Bart knew we were following and he's waiting till we go by. Maybe he heard us and wants to shake us in the fog."

Jo stood still. "No, I don't hear him."

They stood a moment, undecided what to do. Then Will said in a whisper, "Could be he's right near and listening to us. Anyhow, whether or not, why don't we go on? If he should be behind us and catches up with us, we can say that we're on the way to his wharf, that is if it's Black Bart. We can say we want to borrow his skiff, since he was so kind to offer it."

"Okay," whispered Will. "We'll say we want it tomorrow. We wouldn't today. You can't see your hand before your face."

"Let's listen a jif, just to see if the footsteps start up again," Jo said almost at Will's ear.

From the harbor came the sound of a starting outboard, the double tone, *urh-aah*, of Old Growler, the diaphone on Starvation Island. But they could no longer hear footsteps. Then, suddenly, they became aware of stealthy ones approaching from behind them.

"Let's get off the road, quick," said Jo. "Get behind the alders. We'll be near enough to see who passes."

They hopped the ditch running along the road and knelt behind the alder thicket. They weren't too soon. The stealthy steps came near. Soon they would be abreast of them.

CHAPTER SIX

FOOTSTEPS IN THE FOG

A gull, invisible in the fog, floated overhead. *Ha-ha-ha*, its call, like insane laughter, floated down. As if this were a signal, the oncoming footsteps broke into a run. The crouching boys peered through the alder branches.

Then out of the fog emerged a pink dress. It was Lettie! She held the long skirt of her costume off the ground with both hands.

Will and Jo burst from the thicket. She screamed.

"Now, you've done it, now you've let Black Bart know we're trailing him!" said her brother.

"I have not. You did," said Lettie indignantly. "I was just going along minding my own business and you scared the wits out of me. I thought it was Black Bart."

"Well, whosever fault it is, we've probably lost him for good. That scream would warn him to disappear, and fast. Now we'll have no way to prove he was the one in Mary Pete's house if we don't find him leaving it by this road," said Jo.

"If only you'd sung out and let us know it was you coming—" Will gave a little groan of despair.

"How did I know it was you two? I couldn't see in this fog. You might have been Black Bart and a friend for all I could tell."

Then they heard a car coming fast from the direction of the village. They had time only to step down into the ditch when it passed. It was Bart's great black car.

"What in thunder!" exclaimed Jo. "How in the world could he have gotten himself down to his house in this short time?"

"Perhaps it was someone else you saw out that attic window after all," suggested Lettie.

"Maybe he had parked his car in a side road. Maybe he didn't want anyone to hear him drive up to Mary Pete's. There's lots of roads off this one, little wood roads with grass in the middle of them. They don't go anywhere in particular," said Jo.

"Perhaps if we looked along them we'd find tire marks or something to show his car had just been there," said Lettie. "Now help me get out of this strait-jacket dress and I'll help you investigate them."

She backed up to Will and after a bit of fumbling and scowling he was able to free her from the pink garment into the comfort of her blouse and shorts.

"Wait a sec for me, you two. I'll sprint and put the dress in the kitchen so nothing will happen to it," said Lettie.

Will groaned at the delay, but Lettie was already running and, after all, the search idea was hers.

Lettie returned running and they joined her. They found no telltale marks in the first rough little road, nor the next. The third proved to be not much more than a turnaround for cars. The only tire marks here were faint and blurred and an abandoned car, wheelless, windowless, and scarred, glared at them like a death's head from the middle.

Their search of the next road was more fruitful. In its deep ruts they found crisp tire marks and daisies and buttercups flattened but still fresh.

"This is it. This is where Black Bart parked his car," said Lettie jubilantly. "And that proves he's up to some skulduggery. Why in the world didn't he drive right up to the house and knock on the door and sing out like anybody else?"

"It strikes me that now's the time to march on down to his wharf and see what we can find about him. We know he won't be there to cramp our style," said Jo.

"What are we waiting for?" asked Will. "If Black Bart does come back and find us, we can say we want to borrow a skiff. *Now* aren't you glad, Lettie, that I didn't turn him down on his boat offer?"

"No, I'm not," she answered with a toss of her head. "I don't want to be grateful to him for one single solitary thing. Isn't he the one that's wrecking everything for Mary Pete? She's so nice and kind and all. I don't see how he can do it."

Then, not to waste any more of the time Bart was away, they ran all the way to his wharf. His office was in a small building like a first-grader's drawing of a house halfway down the wharf. They went inside and saw that it was both store and office. Its shelves were full of paint cans, lobster plugs, and twine. The room was empty and quiet except for the hum of a red coke machine and the jingle of the wall telephone.

"Good, cokes," said Lettie, brightening. "I'm thirsty as all get out. Come to think of it, though, I don't have a cent."

Will found a quarter in his pocket, and Jo a nickel.

48

Neither coin was right for the slot in the coke machine.

"There must be someone in charge of the store. Let's look for him and get our money changed," said Jo. "Then when we have our cokes we can make them last a long time. That way we can study the place."

They went outside and to the end of the dock. Here over the water the fog was so damp that their hair and clothes were soon beaded with moisture. From the harbor they heard the *tunk-tunk* of someone hammering on the engine of an invisible boat.

Suddenly below them a voice said, "Drat! Why don't I ever get the same weight twice. Contrary-minded, these lobsters. Weigh 'em up, write down the amount, turn 'round, and the scales say something different. Drat the things."

They looked down and saw a float moored to the wharf. On it was a boy of high-school age dipping out lobsters from under the plank floor. He was almost as tall and thin as the dip net he used.

"Are you in charge of the store?" Jo called down to him.

The boy jumped in surprise. "Didn't know anyone was up there!" he exclaimed. "This fog plays tricks on your ears. Ayuh, I'm supposed to be in charge of the store, but Bart has put me to work down here weighing up lobsters for him. Bart, he's gone chasing off somewheres again."

He went on with his work. He brought up the speckly green crustaceans from beneath the float as if there were no end to the supply. The large compartment beneath his feet was awash with sea water and the lobsters dripped with it as he put them in a wire basket on the scales.

"What we want," Jo told him, "is some change for the coke machine."

The boy answered without stopping his work. "See that glass jar with netting 'round it? Hanging down from the top rung of the ladder, it is. Well, lower your money down

49

to me in it. I can make change for you right here. Bart rigged the thing up. When the men start coming in from their hauling all to once, we don't have to keep trotting up and down the ladder to get more money to pay them for their catch."

Will and Jo dropped their coins into the jar and lowered away. The boy replaced them with three dimes. "Take her away," he called up. "Me, I got to get on with this. Bart wants 'em all weighed up. I got to step on it."

Lettie remembered the message that Bart had sent to Mary Pete by way of Ebbie. "I understand Bart is going to have a surprise for everybody on the Fourth," she began as the jar came spinning up at the end of the line.

But before the boy could answer, a powerboat moved in out of the fog and pulled up to the float for gasoline. The moment for discovering more about Bart's surprise had gone.

Jo tipped out the coins and let the jar down once more. "Let's get our cokes," he said.

They went back to the office-shop. Will fed their coins into the red machine. When their bottles emerged with cold-clouded sides, he reminded them, "Make your drinks last a good long time. That way, if anyone comes, we'll have an excuse for being here."

Very carefully they studied the room. If Bart was up to some skulduggery, it didn't show. His desk was almost bare except for a tall spike with sales slips speared on it. There were no notations on his desk calendar which still stood at January. The black safe was shut, and above it the clock ticked, *Wouldn't-you-like-to-know, wouldn't-you-like-to-know.*

Lettie examined the safe. It was decorated with whirls and flourishes in a fine gold line. She gave the thick legs an impatient kick. "Whatever Bart took from Mary Pete's, he'll probably lock it up in here with all his secrets. I mean if he did take something, of course. Isn't this safe just what you would expect him to have? Big and black like his car."

"Yeah," said Will, "I suppose we'd better get going. Don't think we'll learn much here." He tipped back his head to get the last drops from the bottle. Then, almost choking, he cried, "Look," and pointed to the back wall. There over the door was a rifle. It rested upon a pair of wooden arms and its shining stock and bright barrel told that it was more than an ornament.

"We might just as well go home. We'll never find anything more than that gun here," said Lettie.

"*You* can," said her brother. "Me, I'm going down and watch that boy Sim." He started off and the others followed.

They hadn't noticed until they were climbing down the slippery ladder how far below the float was. Nor that it was almost awash. Their extra weight brought sea water oozing up between the floor boards. Their feet were soon soaked through but they scarcely noticed. They were too intent on what they hoped to learn from Sim.

Once more Lettie asked about Bart's Fourth-of-July surprise.

If Sim had heard her question the first time, he gave no sign. As he emptied a netful of dark-green lobsters, their cruel claws shut tight with yellow plastic bands, he said, "I'd be the last fellow to know. Bart, he's a great hand to have schemes a-going. He's always working up something and keeping close as a clam 'bout it till he's good and ready to spill it. H-m-m, now, let's see, that's thirteen pounds more."

"He's got quite a gun up there in his office." Will tried to keep his voice casual. "It's a pretty good one, isn't it?"

" 'Tis," Sim agreed heartily. "It's a whole lot better than

he needs for just scaring off lobster thieves. But then Bart's always a great one for good gear. He says, 'I might as well buy the best while I'm at it.'" It was plain that Sim admired his boss. He looked at the three cousins as if he saw them for the first time. "You Mary Pete's folks that are here for the summer?"

"We're her cousins," was Jo's honest answer.

Before climbing up the ladder, they took one look into the hole from which Sim dipped lobsters. The float was an oversized crate and its water-filled interior was dark with claws, legs, and wispy, waving feelers.

Their talk on the way back was about Bart. Why did he have such a fine gun, they wondered. Why had he sneaked into Mary Pete's house under cover of the fog, when once upon a time he had visited there openly?

Lettie decided to ask Mary Pete if either she or Ebbie had come into the house while the attic costume hunt went on. Until they knew that they couldn't be sure that it was Bart they had heard there. She went to the drugstore as soon as they returned and came to the kitchen to rejoin the boys shaking her head.

"Neither she nor Ebbie was in the house until just a short time ago. Ebbie put wood on the kitchen fire less than an hour ago, she told me. And she says we're crazy if we think that Bart Simes would have been in the house. She says he hasn't for a long time, and would be unlikely to dare to now with the bridge in prospect. And, oh, she's making the most wonderful witches' broth out there. She promised she'd let me help her make another on the first rainy day."

Will ignored Lettie's last remark. "I still believe it was Bart that I saw leaving by the back door, I do. Tonight we must get Mary Pete to look around for something that he might have taken. If he didn't come to see a person, he must have been after a thing."

But their cousin could find nothing missing or out of order when she looked that evening. As for the three here on a week's trial, the thought of telling Mary Pete of this never came into their minds, what with the excitement of getting costumes ready for the next day and wondering about the mysterious visitor.

CHAPTER SEVEN

BART SPRINGS HIS SURPRISE

The Fourth of July began very well.

Sometime during the night the fog had rolled off. Not a shred of its woolly whiteness had been left behind, unless the gauzy cobweb squares spread on the grass and twinkling with red, blue, and green drops were remnants of it. The day was brisk and beautiful.

From the moment of waking, everyone in the old Tibbetts house was too busy with costume preparation to think about Bart and the bridge. Again no one remembered to speak to Mary Pete about a week's trial.

While she and the cousins were hurrying through breakfast, Ebbie came stamping into the kitchen. His arms were piled high with firewood and his chin was held higher to avoid scraping it on rough bark. "Quiet out on the water. Scarcely a ripple. Aren't going to keep the shop shut up all day, be you, Mary Pete?" he asked. From the way he crashed sticks of wood into the box it was plain he disapproved of this.

"Fourth of July, Ebbie." Her rebuke was almost mocking. "Can't I take the day off along with the rest of the folks? Oh, I know as well as you do we're going to have a rush of business before it's over. But it won't come till after dinner when the overeating has been done. Thank goodness, there won't be burns to salve. Not having fireworks these days has done away with that, dull as it is without them. But pies, cakes, doughnuts, and lobster salad will be consumed in large quantities and there's bound to be a need for our remedies. This morning, however, I'm going to lock up the telephone in the shop and forget it. I'm off to the parade. Why don't you turn out for it, too, Ebbie?"

"Rather go to a cat's funeral," was his doleful answer as he left the kitchen.

"He'll be at the parade just the same. He never misses a 'time' nor an event, not Ebbie. Now, you young ones, get busy on your costumes. The band has several places to go and this is one of the first places on their route. Before you know it, you'll hear them striking up at the school ground."

Apparently Mary Pete heard martial music in her head already. She went between table and sink whistling "The Stars and Stripes Forever." When Lettie began to help she said, "Scoot, skedaddle, and get to work on costumes," then went back to her tune.

Before Lettie put on her pink dress, she had to help Jo. He had prepared tin cans by stripping off labels and removing both ends. When he strung them on his arms, large cans at the top, smaller toward his wrists, he was helpless. Although the cans made a splendid clank and jingle he couldn't bend his elbows after they were in place. Lettie must fasten the long seam of the large mock can for him. This was a cardboard cylinder of aluminum-painted cardboard which extended from his armpits almost to his knees. So long was the joining that Mary Pete's scotch tape was almost gone and Lettie was getting very fidgety.

"Botheration!" she exclaimed when for the third time the end of the tape stuck on the roll. "I'm not going to pick that off again. The bottom of this thing of yours is going to be fastened with a safety pin. After all, you *are* a Horrible."

"And I'm a horrible Horrible." Will spoke with satisfaction as he turned away from the kitchen mirror. He had been painting his face, and ferocious frown lines of charcoal and lipstick streaks along his cheeks went oddly with his smiling mouth. His neck was rigid because he had stuck the handle of the feather duster inside his collar.

"You're ready," said Lettie reproachfully. "Go listen at the back door for the band going by. If you see the truck, shout. I'll have to hurry now."

"Okay." Will put Mary Pete's Indian blanket across his shoulders and stationed himself at the back door.

Lettie finished helping Jo. Then she squirmed into the pink dress. Mary Pete was hooking up the back for her when Will called, "Here they come, a whole truckload of them with horns and drums and blazing red uniforms."

"Hurry, Mary Pete, hurry," begged Lettie.

"I can't if you wiggle so," answered her cousin.

Lettie was a statue until the last hook was fastened. Then she tied the strings of an old bonnet trimmed with red roses and settled a lace scarf about her neck and ran. Jo and Will waited at the door. The three hurried off.

Jo pulled Ebbie's ax from the chopping block and settled the tin funnel on his head. Already he was having trouble with his mask which was an encircling cardboard cylinder. It slid about his head and made it difficult to see and breathe.

Lettie, too, had her difficulties. She must lift up her trailing skirts with both hands, hold her breath lest she burst the waist-band, and all the time wear a long-ago and faraway expression proper for her ancient pink gown. Or so she thought until she heard in the distance the squeal of a fife, the roll of a drum. Her heart leaped. "Botheration!" she cried, and hiked up her skirts and ran. The expression on her face was completely here and now.

When the three entrants came panting into the schoolyard, the parade was still waiting. Someone pinned numbers on their backs. The Pink Lady was ushered to the line of Antiques, the Tin Woodsman and the Indian to the ranks of Horribles.

The bandsmen were ready, their peaked caps set straight, high jacket collars hooked. Their shapes and sizes as varied as those of their instruments, they obeyed their leader's signal. *Tootle-tee-tee* from the fife, *thrum-thrum* from the drum, and they were off. Hearts as well as heels responded to the beat and lilt of the music. Down to the wharf and back they marched to the judges waiting on the schoolhouse steps. If the music kept on they would all have marched forever, even Jo, whose mask continued to interfere with seeing and breathing.

The delight of parading was not enough to keep them from being disappointed at the judges' choices for prizes. Mary Pete joined her cousins when the awards had been made to others.

"Just never you mind not winning," she consoled them. "I never won once. Bart and I always came as Horribles and he did win a prize one time."

"He would," said Lettie. "He's a natural-born horrible."

"All the prize I want is being able to wiggle my head again," said Will as he pulled the feather duster handle from his collar.

Jo was speechless until his mask was ripped off. By the time he had slid off his tin bracelets, the three-legged race was being called.

Will and Jo entered and were given a short length of rope to bind themselves together, ankle to ankle. Mary Pete tied a strong knot for them.

"I wonder where Bart is?" Jo asked as she knelt before them. "Don't you remember he said he was springing a surprise today?"

"I do remember," she answered, "and he will. If Bart Simes announces he'll do a thing, he will."

Then with a shout of, "On your marks. Get set. One, two, three, *go!*" the three-legged race was off. Ankle to ankle, arms entwined, the contestants scampered, hitched, and stumbled ahead.

"Keep step, for goodness' sake," Will growled to Jo.

"You do the same," said Jo.

By the time they mastered the art of running as one person, the race was over. They had come in last.

Now they were calling the cracker race, and it was Lettie's turn to compete. She gave her bonnet and scarf to Mary Pete, then hurried to a long table where crackers stood in counted piles.

"First one through and able to whistle clearly one bar of 'America' wins the race," said a judge. "Each one stand before his own pile and no nudging each other."

At the signal Lettie, with a do-or-die expression on her face, began eating crackers. Soon she discovered that it took more than a good appetite to eat speedily. Excitement made her mouth dry, and it was difficult to swallow a pulpy mass of crackers once she had chewed it. However, from the corner of her eyes she saw that she was doing as well as her neighbors. That is until Bart's big black car drove into the schoolyard.

Swallow. Chew. Chew. She saw him swing down a sign from the carrier on his car. *Swallow. Chew. Chew.* Bart leaned the sign against his car. The words *Eden Island Bridge* in bold black letters leaped across the distance. Anger filled her throat and made her jaws refuse to work.

"Come on, Lettie, only three crackers to go. You're ahead now," Jo urged her.

Again she tried to swallow, and once more was unsuccessful. At her elbow came a whistle, slightly muffled by cracker crumbs at first but increasingly clear, "My country 'tis of thee." The race was over. Lettie turned and spit out her mouthful into the long grass. Then, without waiting for comforting or reproaches, she ran toward Bart. The two boys went with her.

By this time Bart had opened a card table and set it up. On it he had placed a pad of paper with a pen across it.

"Come on up, folks, and see the rosy future that lies ahead for our town. Any of you haven't signed our petition for the bridge, here's your chance right now."

With scowling faces the three cousins stared at Bart's sign. A picture below the bold letters showed a concrete-and-steel bridge soaring over a body of water. A line of cars moved along the bridge and beneath it shot jaunty speedboats. Many more craft, some under sail and heeled over, were endangering each other on the water. Riders in cars waved to voyagers and everyone on land and sea was smiling in delight at the existence of this new bridge.

To the three cousins the bridge's setting was all too familiar. That was surely Eden Island at the far end, with the addition of a low, yachty building aflap with flags. At first the near end looked strange. Then they saw that the artist had drawn the bridge supports rising from the very spot where the old Tibbetts house stood. Its gracious façade was bright in the sunlight as they looked from the drawing to it and back.

Afterward Lettie wondered at her outspokenness. Perhaps wearing a costume made her another person for the time.

"You're hateful, Bart Simes," she exploded, to her own surprise.

Then Will, who hadn't wanted to offend Bart before, came out strongly against him. His face, with its streaked Indian war paint, was stern. "You can't do a thing like this to Mary Pete," he said. Then, taking a deep breath, he added, "If your boats were the last ones on earth, I wouldn't borrow one. No, not even if Noah's Flood was here."

Bart's Fourth-of-July surprise had ruined the holiday.

CHAPTER EIGHT

THE OLD COPYBOOK IS MISSING

At the supper table that Fourth-of-July night they could talk about nothing but Bart and the bridge.

"He must have been tearing off to get those old engineer's drawings of his bridge when he went by us in the fog yesterday," said Will.

"Hateful of him, wasn't it?" said Lettie. Then she burst out impetuously, "I think we ought to get a petition of our own. Why should he have things his own way? We should get the names of people like us who positively don't want that bridge."

Mary Pete's little laugh was more sorrowful than gay. "I'm afraid that even if some folks don't in the least want his bridge, they wouldn't dare oppose Bart; they owe him too much money to risk it. Also, some just don't care one way or the other if something that's lovely is ruined. They call it *progress*. That's almost sadder still. Oddly enough, most of those who live out on Eden don't want the bridge. There's a few families on the far side and they don't like the thought of everyone and his brother coming out among them. There, again, some of them owe money to Bart. They're mortgaged up to their necks."

"I thought Bart was a lobster dealer," said Will.

"So he is, but he also sells gear and gasoline on credit and makes a loan to a man who wants a new fishing boat. That way, all in all, he gets himself a good deal of power. If the man whose boat is only partly paid for refused to sign Bart's petition, Bart might decide to take away his boat, don't you see?"

They did, and for some time sat in sober-faced silence. Then Mary Pete stood up from the table and asked in another tone of voice, "Who wants to go goose-grass greening with me tomorrow? It'll do me good to get out and breathe fresh air for a change. Take my mind off this bridge affair, too. In a short while there's going to be a hearing on it to give folks a chance to speak their minds on it. If I get brooding and think about nothing else, when the fatal day of the hearing comes, I may not be able to speak *my* mind. I'll be too upset. Not that I think what I say will make the slightest difference. I have the most dreadful feeling that, hearing or not, the bridge is going through. Now, as I was asking, who's going to keep me company on this goose-grass greening?"

" 'Not I,' said the fly. I'm planning to start work right away on one of your boats, Mary Pete." Will spoke with determination. "I want to get one all watertight and painted and row around to show Mr. Bart that the Tibbetts' boats aren't so bad, after all. He was sure sarcastic about them the day he rescued us."

"I'm with you on that project," said Jo.

"Then it will be you and me that will go greening, Lettie," said Mary Pete.

"Yes," Lettie answered, "but what in the world *are* goose-grass greens?"

62

"Oh, a kind of grass that grows with its feet in salt water for part of the time. People around here cook them up to eat. In fact, some, and I'm one, really have a craving for them at times."

With the next day already planned they could start work early. Ebbie told the boys which skiff needed the least work. They set off to buy caulking cotton and compound at the general store.

Mary Pete left Ebbie in charge of the drugstore and, when the tide was sufficiently low, she and Lettie started their greening expedition. The work was very pleasant, Lettie soon discovered, with the sun on their backs and a good salt smell from the marsh where the greens grew. Soon their two grain sacks bulged with the plants.

Mary Pete led the way to a huge log which some winter storm had left to bleach among the grasses. They sat astride the trunk and picked over the greens. Soon Lettie's fingers were flying as fast as her cousin's as they tweaked off root ends and pulled out ramrod-like blossom stems.

The tide turned and came murmuring in close to their feet. Swallows swooped past as they skimmed the water for insects. A song sparrow called *sweet-sweet*. Lettie knew why Mary Pete liked to go greening.

Best of all, the work did not interfere with talk.

Mary Pete said that the plant may have been called goose-grass because the blades were like goose tongues, or perhaps because these birds enjoyed them. "I'll show you the old recipe for them in the copybook I told you about. It's the one that has writing in it about the Indians and their hullabaloos. I do want you to see it," said Mary Pete.

"Who in the world dared to eat these greens the first time?" asked Lettie.

"No one knows for sure, I guess. My grandmother used to tell of the starving time the early settlers had here. Clams or starve, was all. Maybe the Indians told them the greens were good. My grandfather taught me a lot that his grandmother learned from the Passamaquoddy people about herbs and roots and such. I suppose I'm an old-fashioned nut, but in spite of my training in the city as a druggist, I still have great faith in the plants we can gather here."

Lettie liked this serious talk, and having her cousin treat her as if she were the same age. Then, too, thinking of the old days here sent pleasant prickles chasing up her back. How exciting it was and how real! If only such things happened nowdays, like having to live on clams and eat what savages taught you was good.

"Mary Pete," she asked after a thoughtful pause, "are the bunches of dried stuff hanging in the attic part of what you're talking about?"

Her cousin nodded. "I've got them all tagged so I can send Ebbie up for what I need in a hurry. Of course he doesn't know peppermint from tansy but he can read the tags, if barely. Ebbie never was a scholar."

"Maybe I could get them down from the attic when you need them." Lettie's voice was eager. If anyone had reminded her of being here on a week's trial, she might have looked surprised.

By the time they shouldered their sacks to return home, the tide had moved in a good deal. Water inched up among the roots of sea lavender near their old log. It completely covered the route they had traveled in their greening. They must return another way.

If they had not done so, they might have seen something which later would solve a mystery. As it was, they struck inland directly behind the driftwood log and their view of the house and shop was cut off by a screen of alders.

At the end, their route took them out of thickets onto the main road. On both sides Mary Pete pointed out plants with the enthusiasm of a discoverer. She darted from one to another, dipping down to pick a leaf here, a blossom there.

She picked a whole plant and put it on one of Lettie's palms. "That's sundew," she explained, "and the little sticky drops on its hairy leaves are to catch insects to devour."

Then she pointed to another plant with cool lavender cups of blossom. "Wild geranium. I must remember to dig some of their roots. They make a gentle tonic for some of my tender old ladies."

Sniffing plants, tasting leaves, Mary Pete would have taken the rest of the morning to travel the short distance home if Ebbie hadn't cut short their pleasant progress.

He spotted them from the shop door and came loping toward them. "For the love of Mike, hurry up, will you? Telephone's been going a steady jingle. All the folks you expected to call yesterday on account of their digestions is calling today, seems as if. I tried to take down their messages but more'n likely got 'em all bolloxed up. Most generally do. It makes me nervous to think of all the poisoning you could do if I got 'em wrong. I wish you'd come and ring 'em all back and ask what they want."

"Okay, okay, Ebbie, I will. Thanks for holding the fort. I've had a lovely morning. Now I'll catch up on those messages of yours. Lettie, will you take our greens and put them to soak in a washtub for me?"

Lettie carried the goose-grass sacks to the kitchen. She hummed as she spilled them out into a washtub and vigorously pumped water onto them. Then she decided to surprise the boys at the boathouse with a picnic lunch.

They were pleased to see her arrive with food and she spread the sandwiches on a sawhorse.

"Wasn't that some yacht that came in?" Will asked her.

"What yacht? I've been too busy to notice," Lettie asked through a mouthful of peanut-butter sandwich.

"Just cast your eye toward Friend Bart's wharf and you'll see her. She must have come into the harbor for gas. Anyhow, she's a dandy yawl, all spit and polish. In fact, just the kind of boat I'm going to have someday myself," said Will. "If only we had this old skiff done, we could row over and really look her over."

"I shouldn't think you'd want to hang around over *there*," his sister reproved him as she glared toward Bart's wharf. "Well, I must say, it's a beautiful boat. It belongs to someone very rich."

Before their lunch was eaten, they saw the sailboat move into mid-harbor under power.

"Just our luck," said Jo. "Off she goes before we really get a good look at her."

But the yawl had not departed. Soon she was tied up at a mooring buoy, a tempting sight to land-based boys. Their work seemed more humdrum than before. "Ho-hum, caulking a skiff gets pretty monotonous," said Jo. "The rate we're going, it'll be several days before we get out on the water. In the meantime, all we can do is admire the yawl from here."

"A cat can look at a king," said Lettie cheerfully.

Will give her a stern look. "How about pitching in? Or are you and Mary Pete going gadding again?"

"We weren't gadding, we were greening. I thought someone ought to accept her invitation. She seems awfully lonely, somehow. I can help you now," she answered.

Will handed her a putty knife. Soon they were all absorbed in work until the roar of Bart's powerful outboard motor interrupted.

"There goes His Nibs," said Jo.

They watched Bart's skiff planing toward the yawl. He

stopped alongside and a man aboard leaned down to take Bart's line while he climbed aboard.

"Did you ever!" Jo burst out. "The owner is a friend and expected him, you can see that. The yawl came in for something beside gas. I bet she belongs to a politician from all Mary Pete has told us about Bart's hobnobbing with them."

With the turning of the tide, the sailboat obeyed its tug. The cousins could plainly read the name *Elmira* in brass letters as she swung at her mooring.

"If she were mine, I'd give her a prettier name than that," said Will. He sighed and pulled another length of caulking cotton from the roll. Rather grimly work went on.

That evening, when they went up the slopes for supper, Will kept turning to admire the *Elmira*. Her slender spars cut the pink sky as she rocked at the mooring. He asked Mary Pete the moment he saw her, "Did you cast your eyes on that yacht out there? Some boat."

"Oh, the *Elmira*? Sure have, and it's not the first time. She was in last summer. If you ask me, whoever it is that owns her is the fellow that gave Bart all his silly ideas. Right after he came, so they tell me, Bart could talk of nothing but a new bridge, a lobster pound, a marina. I must say, I'm not surprised to see the yawl here again." Mary Pete spoke without turning her head. She was searching for something on the kitchen shelf, head tipped back and eyes following her moving index finger. "I can't understand where that copybook has got to, the old one that tells about cooking goose-grass greens. I want Lettie to read it. Have any of you been looking at it?"

No one had been.

"I do remember your speaking about that other writing in it, the part that tells about Indians and hullabaloos and all. I haven't seen it, though," said Lettie.

"I just can't imagine where it can be. I haven't used it

for a coon's age, but it's been here on this shelf right along. Ebbie wouldn't touch it, I'm sure. He keeps away from reading and writing."

"Must be what Bart took when he came in that foggy day," said Jo half-joking. The sharpness of Mary Pete's answer startled him.

"*Bart!* You kids certainly have that man on the brain! Why can't you talk about someone else? Why would he bother with our crumbly old book? Besides, you would see Bart coming out of any house in town but this. A few years ago we had, well, a sort of spat, I guess you'd call it. He announced he was never going to set foot in this house again. He never has. At first it seemed strange without him because always before he'd been in and out like one of the family. However, as you see, we get along fine without Mr. Bart."

"What did you and Bart fight about?" asked Lettie. Then something in her cousin's expression made her add quickly, "Or is that too personal?"

Mary Pete's answer was a curt, "Yes."

They talked a bit more about the copybook's disappearance but, by the next day, no one remembered it. So many disturbing events came crowding in that this mystery was forgotten.

CHAPTER NINE

THE RED FLAGS

The alarm which woke Will the next morning was the sound of hammering, a woody *tunk-tunk*. He got up and when he leaned out of his window, he saw two men in the dooryard. One carried alder and birch saplings, trimmed of leaves and twigs and sharpened to a point, across his shoulder. The other drove them into the ground with the butt end of an ax. Then he tied a ragged strip of turkey-red cotton onto each stake.

Will knew at once what these men were doing. He had often seen such bright markers moving ahead of construction into fields and woods and yards. Devastation always followed at their heels. Forest giants toppled and were burned on the spot, buildings tumbled into heaps of rubble. These flags marked the beginning of the end for the old Tibbetts homestead.

Barefooted, not stopping for a bathrobe, Will ran to Mary Pete's room in the main house. He knocked gently at her door and called, "Mary Pete, Mary Pete."

There was no answer, but sounds from the kitchen told

him where his cousin was. He ran down the back stairs and found her poking fiercely at the fire in the black range.

Will began, "Those men—"

"Oh, I know," said Mary Pete, "but what in the world can I do about it? I never expected anything like this to happen until after the hearing. But I suppose the engineers will have to submit plans and bridge costs then. To do this they will have to study the site and the lay of the land. Oh, I can understand that all right. I guess I wouldn't be minding this disturbance so much if only one of the men had had the courtesy to knock on the door and say, 'Sorry, lady, this is just to let you know we're taking the first step in the destruction of your house, not that we want to inconvenience you in any way, of course.' But they just went ahead without a word as if this land my family has owned time out of mind was no longer ours."

Mary Pete was not the weeping type, but now her eyes sparkled as if they were awash with tears.

"They can't do this! It's still your house, isn't it?" Will stamped a cold bare foot. "I'm going out there now and pull those flags right up by the roots!" If he could feel so angry about a place he had known but a few days, how much more disturbed must Mary Pete be? This house had always been her home.

"Oh, what's the use, Will? What if you did pull them up? Someone else would only drive in some more eventually. My, this smoky fire does make my eyes smart." She dabbed at them with a crumpled paper handkerchief and sniffed. "Let's leave the old stakes there. Maybe they'll serve some useful purpose like making people feel so sorry for me they'll come to the hearing and speak out against the bridge."

"Well, I'll go wake up the others. They'll want to see the dastardly work going on," said Will.

"You can tell 'em that I'm about to rustle up a big breakfast for us all. We'll eat together and cheer each other up. I'm so glad you're all here. It would be dreary with just Ebbie around. He'd say, 'Well, Mary Pete, I dunno what,' when he saw the red flags, and that would be the extent of his help."

Will roused the others. He showed them the men at work beside the house.

"The 'Down-with-Black-Bart Society' hasn't accomplished very much, has it?" Lettie mourned.

"After all, we haven't been here long. Our seven days' trial isn't up yet. We must get busy," said Jo.

Will frowned, "Things are going ahead much faster than Mary Pete expected. We've got to do something before the hearing."

"Probably those politicians she talks about have already decided to build their old bridge anyway, no matter what anyone says at the hearing," said Jo.

Mary Pete called up the back stairs, "Two minutes and breakfast will be ready. Rise and shine. It's sausages."

"Be there soon," Lettie answered.

"Look," said Will firmly, seizing each by an elbow, "no matter what, we've got to get a list of names of people who don't want this bridge."

"Remember what Mary Pete said about people in Bart's power not signing," Lettie reminded him.

He ignored this remark. "Look, Let, Jo and I have got to work on that skiff. We'll need it more than ever now. We want to row out to Eden Island and get the people there who don't want the bridge to sign our petition. What's more, it'll be much easier to keep tabs on Friend Bart if we have a boat. So, you see, it's up to you to start out today after names."

"No, I don't see," she answered. "Besides, I'm shy about talking to strangers. You know that."

"Oh, my foot, if you're shy I'd hate to meet a lion some-day," said her brother.

"We've got to hurry. Breakfast must be ready. Let's settle this by drawing lots for the job," Jo suggested.

Lettie fumbled in her bathrobe pocket for a piece of paper to tear into strips. She drew out a card and, without looking at it, made two tears across it. She shortened one of the three pieces that this had made. Then she arranged them in her folded hand to look of equal length.

"Quick, draw!" she ordered.

The boys obeyed. Jo groaned at finding his piece the shortest. When Lettie looked at her strip of card she realized what she had done. This was no ordinary card but one she had brought from home—her S.O.S. card, she called it. Her mother had addressed it to herself and given it to Lettie. "If at the end of the first week with Mary Pete you don't want to stay, mail this to me. I will understand and drive down to bring you home."

At that time the card was very important to them. Now the thought of having destroyed it hardly mattered, or wouldn't until she had more time to think about it.

The three cousins scattered to dress and two minutes later were eating scrambled eggs and sausage. Outside, the *tunk-tunk* of stake driving continued. They raised their voices to drown out that hateful sound.

When Mary Pete left for the shop, the others looked out the kitchen window. The line of stakes extended almost to the shore now. The bits of torn turkey-red tied on them blew out like flags.

"Makes me think of those miniature golf courses where people go to knock out golf balls," said Jo. "What a terrible thing to do to such a dignified old house, stick in all those whippersnapper flags."

74

Then Jo had an idea. I'm going to pull one of the things up and take it with me when I start after names. I'll knock on a door and say, 'Lady, how'd you like to wake up and find someone pounding this into your lawn? How would you like to discover that your house was about to be torn down?' "

A crash of firewood in the box behind the stove interrupted Jo's speech.

Lettie jumped and gave a little shriek. "Ebbie, you ought to give some warning that you're coming."

"Did," Ebbie answered. "Cleared my throat and wiped my feet hard, but you three were thicker'n thieves over there by the window."

"Would you have time to look at the work we've done on the skiff so far?" Will asked Ebbie.

"I guess so. Might even be able to go down and help you a bit unless Mary Pete starts hollering for me to run an errand."

"Golly Moses," said Jo, who was still at the window, "there goes the *Elmira*. Her mainsail's up and she's leaving her mooring."

"If she's going for good we'll never have a chance to check on—" Will had been going to say, "check on Bart's skulduggery and that friend of his," but he remembered in time that Ebbie "half-liked" Bart, as Mary Pete said. He said, instead, "a chance to look her over."

Ebbie sniffed. "I guess you'll find she'll be back soon enough. Don't imagine they'll more than run out 'round the island and take a look at Smuggler's Cove that used to be mine. That fine friend o' Bart's thinks it's a place with great possibilities. He never said what for."

He assured Will that he would meet him soon at the boathouse. Then he went off and Jo turned to writing out the petition that was like Bart's first except that in each sentence he wrote a large black NOT in capital letters. This turned the meaning around completely.

Lettie laughed when she read it. "That's the stuff, Jo," she said. "Let's keep it a secret from Mary Pete until we have a good long list of names." Then she hurried off to work in the drugstore.

Soon after Ebbie returned and pronounced himself a free man. He and Will set out for the boathouse.

Will couldn't know that this day begun with humdrum work was to end in danger. Perhaps, he thought later, if digging out old putty hadn't proved so dull, the turn of events would have been quite different.

CHAPTER TEN

A DREAM COME TRUE TURNS INTO A NIGHTMARE

I wouldn't change places with anyone, Will thought as he began work on the skiff that morning. Everything around him seemed to be free and in motion. Through the open boathouse door he saw dancing waves, soaring sea birds, waving grasses. Even Ebbie, usually so still, was moving constantly. He had forgotten his offer of help and circled the overturned skiff, 'round and 'round, till Will felt dizzy.

"Kind of pretty day out, ain't it?" Ebbie observed after he had run out of advice. "Don't know but what I might row out to the island."

Will's only answer was a fiercer chink of hammer on caulking iron.

"Well, I declare, first thing you know you'll be ready to putty that crack, rate you're going," Ebbie said, still circling. "Yes, sir, guess that's what I'll do, row out to the island. Mary Pete don't want me 'round, that's plain. She's got Lettie answering the phone with one hand and mixing

77

up some of them slops of hers with the other. That's women for you, Will. One minute they need you so bad you can't stir, next minute they're shooing you out the door like an old broody hen. Yes, sir."

He made another complete circle around the skiff.

"Ebbie, would you oblige me by walking in the opposite direction? It makes my head spin 'round when you always go the same way," said Will.

Ebbie reversed. "Say, why don't you knock off a spell and come out to the island with me? Do you good. We won't stay long and you'll have a chance to see the place. Smuggler's Cove is real pretty. It was named for my grandfather Eben. He was a kind of smuggler, you might say, 'though not to amount to much. Anyhow, you ought to see it before Bart gets to prettifying it with red umbrellas and searchlights and such. Come on, what say we go out there on the water and bob around together?" Ebbie said.

Will changed the subject to avoid such temptations. "Tell me, what do you call those sea birds out there so thick near the whirlpool?"

"Them, they're sea geese, or so we calls 'em. Some say they're phalaropes," Ebbie answered.

"I was going out to check on them that day we took the dory and had to be rescued. In the excitement I forgot all about the birds," said Will. He chinked away in silence for a time. Then the sparkle on the water proved too much to resist. "Okay, Ebbie, let's go to your island for a quick visit."

Will hadn't really planned to give in. Now that he had, he soothed his conscience by thinking that he might find some clue to Bart's behavior on the island and followed Ebbie out to the beach. Together they pushed Ebbie's skiff to the water.

They were afloat in the skiff when they heard Mary Pete

calling Ebbie. She was running down the boathouse path and beckoning frantically. Even stolid Ebbie heard the urgency in her voice. He gave a little growl and beached the skiff again.

"That's a woman for you, changeable as April weather. *Now* she wants me." Ebbie strode off.

Will returned to work. He should have been glad that he hadn't gone off with Ebbie. He wasn't. He couldn't keep his eyes from straying to Ebbie's skiff. Half in, half out of the water, with oarlocks set and oars resting in them it was an inviting sight. It seemed to call him with the words Ebbie had used, "come on, what say we go out there on the water and bob around together?"

Will was able to resist this call until he saw the yawl returning. That settled it. He'd make a quick trip out to inspect the *Elmira* at her mooring. He might not have another chance to study the yacht's elegant lines at such close range.

He untied Ebbie's skiff and pushed off. Ebbie might know how to fix up a skiff but he neglected his own, Will discovered. The little boat badly needed paint and leaked so much that three inches of water lay in the bottom. As for the oars, one blade had split and almost half of it was missing. Will saw these details without thinking about them. His thoughts were on the *Elmira*.

Last night he had dreamed about the yawl and now he continued that dream in his mind. He had become her captain and was winging toward Spain. Midway in this imaginary voyage he saw that the *Elmira* was not making for her mooring but Bart's wharf. He followed her.

He hoped that no one saw him as he rowed alongside the yawl at the dock. Sim, Bart's young helper, was not about. Bart and his friend were too busy with mooring lines to notice anything else. Confident that he hadn't been observed. Will nosed the skiff under the lobster wharf. He was thankful the boat was cockelshell enough to squeeze between the closely spaced log pilings. Once under the dock he quietly shipped the oars and laid them across the gunnels. Then he waited.

He felt very safe in this dusky place under the dock. It was like being in a cave. Soon two pairs of feet thudded along the boards directly over his head. Will smiled to think of how secret his hideout was.

Bart's voice was the first he heard. "You can take over now. The office is all yours, Sim. Don't get too far from that phone. I told you I was expecting a call from Ned White, remember? He said he was going to let me know when to expect the lobster truck but he hasn't called yet. When he does, tell him the lobsters are ready for him. I promised Harry here one of Mrs. Trafton's spaghetti feeds. That's what we're going for now. You stick around, boy."

If Sim answered, Will didn't hear him. A nod or wave as Bart went by the office window might have sufficed as reply.

The footsteps overhead died away. Will hugged himself with crossed arms. It was cool here out of the sun. And Bart's words had given him a shivery feeling of anticipation. They offered him the chance he had hoped for, the opportunity to explore the *Elmira*.

Spaghetti feed, Bart had said. If he ate spaghetti as slowly as Will he would be gone for quite some time. With the sprinkling and mixing of grated cheese, the slow wrapping of strands around a fork that must be done, Will could have ample time to carry out his plan undetected.

For a bit longer he sat motionless. Sim might take it into his head to look aboard the yawl himself. Although the *Elmira* had come into the harbor last year, Sim might not have had a good chance to poke about in the cabin. So Will waited. The only sounds he heard were the *drip-drip* of pilings as water from the receding tide drained down them and the *slap-slap* of small waves nibbling at the sailboat's sun-dappled sides.

Finally Will decided the moment to move had come. He reached out and seized one of the log pilings. He pulled the boat from one piling to the next, a quieter method than rowing with its thumps and splashes.

As the skiff moved close to the yawl, he wondered if he was doing something criminal. Was this trespassing or boat breaking or what?

He balanced this thought against what Bart was doing to Mary Pete. Then he felt no hesitation. Just think, not an arm's length away might be some proof of Bart's wrong-doing.

Will stood carefully on the rower's seat. Yes, he could easily swing up over the rail and aboard the yawl. He tied Ebbie's skiff on a short line, snubbed close to the piling so that the little boat was well out of sight beneath the wharf. That way, if he should need to leave the *Elmira* in a hurry the skiff was nearby. Then he swung himself aboard the yawl.

It was all so easy that he couldn't quite believe he had done it. He stared at the mahogany grating beneath his feet. He touched the steering wheel, and its bright spokes were warm beneath his fingers. At last he was on the *Elmira* just as he had been in his dream last night.

He gave himself a shake. There's work to be done; I'm not here just to make my dreams come true, he thought. At any moment a lobster boat might be nudging up to the wharf. That would bring Sim down on the run to sell gas or buy lobsters. He doubted whether the boy could see Ebbie's skiff but he might catch Will aboard the yawl.

Will must hurry. He tried the companionway door. It was bolted shut but not locked. This was good luck. Cautiously he shot the bolt and opened the double doors. Then he carefully shut them behind him.

From the companionway steps he glanced about the cabin. Here was everything that the boat of his dreams must have. A neat Shipmate stove, four good bunks with leatherette-covered mattresses, rolled charts resting on crosspieces overhead. A ship's clock was about to strike half-past eleven, and then did it, *ping-ping, ping-ping, ping-ping-ping*, the little brass hammer striking the brass bell above the clock face. He admired the small icebox and the tiny sink beneath it. With approval he counted the storage lockers. He even tried the brass pull on the door of a locker which was forward above a bunk. It opened the door smoothly. Empty, the whole cupboard, that shows there's room enough and to spare aboard here.

For these first minutes the *Elmira* was as good as his. He stroked the mast rising through the center of the cabin. His delighted smile embraced the entire cabin.

Now he must get to work. After all, he hadn't come here just to admire. Where to begin? Perhaps the rolled charts overhead might give some hint of what Bart and his friend were up to. There might be notations on margins or even secret papers rolled inside them for hiding.

He took the charts down, one at a time, and spread them on a bunk. He studied four and found nothing that had not been printed in a government office. So far, each was a chart of Canadian waters lying not far beyond the border of Maine. He put back the fourth paper roll. His fingers closed about a fifth just as he heard the thud of feet on deck and Bart's voice.

"Mrs. Trafton's kettle is still too hot to set down anywhere," he said. "Open the door for me and I'll put it on your galley stove. That way it won't ruin your varnish job."

The spaghetti dinner was to be eaten aboard! Will should have thought of that.

He had only a moment for deciding. Should he burst out of the cabin at once and bluster an excuse about coming to admire the *Elmira*? Bart would wonder why he hadn't asked permission. Should he duck down and try to hide until the meal was eaten? This was the more cowardly course, or was it? He could learn a great deal from eavesdropping, dangerous as it might be.

As these thoughts flashed through Will's mind, he remembered the empty locker. Its length he wasn't sure of; it had tapered off into shadows where the bow came to a point. He opened the door. It was wide enough. Feet first, he jumped in. While he slid forward, he reached his arms above his head and quickly shut the door. Not tight, of course; he must leave a slight crack for breathing and for listening.

Before he stretched his legs as far as they could go, feet pounded on the companionway ladder, a metal pot banged down, and Bart spoke.

"Thanks for casting us off, Sim. Expect us when you see us. Stick around until every last lobster gets loaded aboard that truck. Keep your eyes open. So long."

As he spoke the engine throbbed. Will felt vibrations even in his far corner. The *Elmira* was under way, and carrying him in a very different fashion from the cruise in his dream. Here he was like a frightened rabbit in his dive hole. How long could he remain undiscovered? If the men didn't open the locker and find him here, would he have the courage to lie low until they returned?

CHAPTER ELEVEN

THE GREEN FOOTPRINT

Afterward both Jo and Lettie blamed themselves for being too busy to look out toward the boathouse. During the morning that Will disappeared, Jo's mind was on gathering names and Lettie was immersed in her work with Mary Pete. The thought that Will might be in any danger was the farthest from their minds.

Before Jo hurried off to start his work, he asked Lettie to be the first to sign their petition. She boldly wrote her name in full, hoping that it looked like a grown-up signature.

Jo rolled up the sheet when the ink was dry. "Don't tell Mary Pete, will you, that I pulled up one of the stakes with a red flag. I put a clothespin in the ground to mark the exact spot. That way I can put it back and we won't need to worry if its against the law or something to move it."

Lettie nodded. "I shan't tell her, you bet." She watched Jo start off with the engineer's flag across a shoulder and the rolled petition in his hand. "You look like one of those men on the state seal. You know the kind I mean, an oar in one hand, an ax in the other. Try your best to get heaps of names, won't you?"

"Hundreds," he called back. "I want to make up for not finding any evidence in the Indian shell heap. Well, see you."

Jo's speech was reassuring. Lettie went lightheartedly to the shop. Soon she forgot everything but the pleasure of working for Mary Pete.

Soon Mary Pete said to Ebbie, "It's a lovely day, the kind that always makes you want to be out there on Eden. Why don't you take a run out there, have a little holiday for yourself? Lettie can help me."

Ebbie's rocking chair by the window had been tipping back and forth with the regularity of a patent machine. "Me, a holiday?" Ebbie turned a surprised face to Mary Pete.

"Sure," she answered. "Can't remember when you had one of your own, not the national kind."

"Oh, all right," he said. Reluctantly he dragged himself from the window where he had settled to watch the world in comfort.

Mary Pete winked at Lettie as Ebbie marched slowly off. When the door closed after him, she burst out, "Poor old Ebbie! He does try, of course, but you can do everything he does and better, I'm sure. What a blessed relief to have a holiday from his old stories. I've heard 'em all a million times. Mention herring to Ebbie (and I don't advise it), and out comes the tale of Billy Balch who put his net across Smuggler's Cove to trap the herring in there. When the tide went down it left barrels and barrels of the fish stranded out of water. The smothered herring lay in windrows on the bottom and their oil covered the harbor so that there wasn't so much as a ripple on it all summer. See,

I know every word of his stories. Today let's forget them and have us a good time." She gave Lettie a warm hug, and added, "I didn't know how lonesome I was until you three came."

Lettie grinned. It was good to be wanted. She pushed the thought of their staying only a week back in her mind. "Don't forget, you're going to make me work," she said.

"Go study my shelves in the shop. That's the first step in learning this business. I'll keep on with this job and if the phone rings, will you answer for me? Say I'm busy. Take down the message completely. When I answer, I have to listen to all aches and pains, past and present. You may be spared that."

"Do you mind if I take one of your horehound drops, Mary Pete? I'll bring you one, too. I remember where you keep them." Lettie parted the curtain that shut off the back room and went into the shop. She took down from the shelf the candy jar and set it on the counter by the scales with their brass pans. She popped a drop into her mouth and gave one to Mary Pete. Then she returned to study the stock.

On three sides were rows of square crystal bottles with ground-glass stoppers. Each had its contents named on a white label outlined in gold. Under these were pasted paper labels. The writing on these, brown with age and antique with its flourishes, told from where each ingredient had come. This small store on the coast of Maine had received drugs and condiments from all over the world.

Lettie saw seeds, pods, and powders, syrups, roots, and barks. Their colors ranged from scarlet to dull brown, their shapes from the star of anise seeds to rough bark rolls of sassafras. Lettie read the labels aloud. The names were like the incantations of a magician. Some of the place names Lettie had never heard of. Her thoughts went winging off as she read them. Mary Pete's goods had been brought across the seven seas and from six continents.

Agar agar from Japan, *orris fingers* from Spain, *gum acacia* from Egypt and *cochineal bugs* from Brazil, *quassia chips* from Panama, *Irish moss* from Scituate, *calabar beans* from Africa, *nutgalls* from Persia, *cinchona bark* from South America, *nux vomica buttons* from India, she chanted. On and on she moved, her eyes moving along the shelves. Sometimes she lifted a stopper to sniff, sometimes she peered closer to be sure she was really seeing a particular name. *Job's tears*, for instance, that looked like gray beads for stringing. *Jequirity seeds* from India had a written note of caution below the name, "One will kill a cow." A glowing red powder was labeled *Dragon's blood* from China. If she lifted the lid would a fire-breathing creature sweep out into the room like a genie from a bottle? That stopper she did not lift.

B-r-r, b-r-r, b-r-r. The telephone brought Lettie back from the Orient.

"Three rings, that's us, I'm afraid," called Mary Pete.

Lettie ran to the back room. The mouthpiece of the wall telephone was so high that she had to turn it down to speak. "Hello, hello," she called, standing on tiptoe with a pencil in her hand. She hoped her voice didn't sound as quavery as she felt. Like Ebbie, she could bollox things up. "Yes, this is Mary Pete's— Well, she's awfully busy now measuring things, you know— Yes, she asked me to take the message— Mrs. Trafton, yes— Usual stomach remedy." She repeated the words that crackled out and wrote them on the pad of paper beneath the telephone. "Spaghetti tonight so you want to have on hand some of Mary Pete's medicine because that Italian stuff always gives you heartburn something terrible. Yes, yes, I'll tell her, Mrs. Trafton. Good-by."

Lettie hung up the receiver and sighed.

"No need to tell me any of it," said her cousin. "I heard every word, sharp as a knife in my ear. Poor Mrs. Trafton, why does she eat that stuff if it does such dreadful things to her? Just because she makes spaghetti for Bart and his yacht-owning friend is no reason she has to eat it. It hurts her sense of thrift not to, I guess. She says herself she squeezes every penny twice." Mary Pete held a glass beaker to the light. "Well, Lettie, here's your chance to go up attic for me. Bring me the bunch of dried *mentha aquatica* that's hanging there, will you? I'll just check that prescription before you go. I'm a bit rusty. Mrs. T. is one of a few that still uses that dose."

Mary Pete slid open a drawer and ran her fingers along the cards inside until she found the one she wanted. "Yes, that's right. Water mint (that's *mentha aquatica*,) one ounce, marsh marigold, one ounce, wild sage, ditto, ginger, one half teaspoon," she read. "As I recall, the bunch of *mentha aquatica* is hanging nearest the stairs on the right-hand side."

Lettie, feeling very useful, hurried off. She felt gay, too, until she reached the foot of the formal stairway. Then she remembered the family ghost, the woman with a red shawl over her head who toiled up these stairs and lifted the drawer handles of a bureau. She paused here a moment. Of course, she told herself, I don't believe in ghosts, not the least bit. But her head was afloat with words like "haunted," and a "mysterious knocking." For a moment she hesitated, then she ran up the dignified staircase like a frightened colt. She paused for a breath at the foot of the attic stairs, then she pounded up their ladder-like steepness.

At the top she cautiously opened the door. The floor boards creaked as if someone had just stepped on them. Garments hanging from the rafters stirred in a slight breeze as if that someone had just slipped behind one to hide. The dressmaker's dummy in a corner had the air of knowing some grim and unhappy fact.

She turned to the right hand, as Mary Pete had suggested, and started her hunt for the *mentha aquatica*. The tag on the first dried bunch read *blue vervain*. She reached for the next and turned it to read *mullein*. The next was labeled *catnip*.

She looked at most of them before she found the label she wanted. Good, she thought. She tried to loosen the string that tied the dried bunch to a nail. A strong jerk and nothing happened. Then she realized that the same little breezes stirring the garments had spun the bunches on their strings until they were twisted tight. Even on tiptoe she couldn't free her bunch.

Then she remembered seeing a bottomless chair on the day of the costume search. It was in a far, dark corner. She made herself bring it from the shadows and place it beneath the *mentha aquatica* bunch.

She mounted the chair frame, a foot straddled on either side, a hand on a rung of the ladderback. As she steadied herself she looked down through the bottomless seat. There in the scatterings of dried leaves a footprint on bare board stood out. It was perfectly outlined, as if it had been made while the leaf shower fell.

Suppose the person who stood there is still up here with me?

The attic door which had been ajar shut with a click. Lettie went rigid with panic. *I'm alone with that person,* she thought.

Once more she reassured herself by speaking aloud. "If there's anyone here, just stay hidden till I get out," she called to the dark corners.

With both hands she gave a terrific tug on the string. It

broke with such suddenness that herbs, Lettie, and bottomless chair all sprawled on the floor. She jumped up quickly and set the chair straight. Then she saw that the footprint had been destroyed. Its precise shape had gone. Untidy heaps of green leaf filled the spot.

But in Lettie's mind the footprint was still sharp and clear . . . about as long as her own foot but very narrow and pointed of toe. *Old-fashioned*, she thought. And then, *Ghosts don't make footprints.*

She picked up the bunch of *mentha aquatica* and fled the attic.

It wasn't until she reached the pleasant, familiar kitchen that she drew a good breath. She stopped here for a moment to allow any look of fright on her face to disappear. Then she walked at a normal pace to the shop.

Mary Pete looked up from her work as Lettie entered. "Good girl, thank you," she said. "But this isn't the one I wanted."

"The tag says so," Lettie said stoutly.

"So it does, and in my own handwriting. However, this plant is no mint. It doesn't have a square stem nor opposite leaves. Could one of the tags have come off on the day you were digging out costumes up there and been put back on the wrong bunch?" Mary Pete asked.

"None of us touched the herbs," said Lettie; "we were much too busy."

"I guess I better go up there and see what's what. In this business of mine I must be careful. I don't think I'm likely to poison anyone but I could make someone uncomfortably ill by not taking care. Will you stay and answer the phone if it rings and keep stirring this mixture on the stove, too? I don't want the stuff to boil over." Mary Pete pointed to the long-handled spoon in the pot and hurried to the attic.

When she returned she wore a puzzled expression. "I don't understand it. The tags are switched around in the craziest fashion. I'm going to call Ebbie and ask him about this mix-up. I hope he hasn't got it into his head that something like this is a good prank to play on me."

Lettie kept her vigil and Mary Pete gave Ebbie a hail.

Ebbie responded to Mary Pete's call. He sauntered into the shop wearing a slightly superior look, as if to say, Well, I guess you couldn't get along without me, after all.

That expression changed to one of injured dignity when he heard why he had been recalled. "Me go switching 'round those tags of yours? Now why would I bother with a fool thing like that?"

"That's exactly it, why would you, or anyone else? I'll ask the boys when they come in about this. No harm has been done to any customer but it could have been. In the meantime I'll get to work on Mrs. Trafton's remedy. Will you pound up some of these leaves in the mortar for me, Lettie? Notice how different they are from those you brought downstairs; you can understand why I was surprised at what the tag read."

Lettie nodded. At the moment she was more interested in the size of Ebbie's feet than in the shape of leaves. She had not observed before how large they were for his moderate-sized body. It was certainly not Ebbie who had made that narrow footprint in the carpet of dry green leaves.

Ebbie turned his rocker away from the window as if to say, if I can't get out to Eden, I don't want to look at the island.

Toward noon Jo came into the shop.

"Kind of dragging your tail feathers, aren't you?" was Ebbie's greeting.

"Hungry," answered Jo.

To Mary Pete's question about his knowledge of the

tag switching he gave such a startled, "I don't know anything about it," that it could not be doubted.

"I'm going over and make myself a sandwich," he announced. He gave Lettie an urgent look to say "Come over soon."

When she had pounded up all the mint, Lettie went to join Jo. She found him deep in the dumps. So far, not one person had signed their petition, except for Lettie.

"Mary Pete was right. She knows the people here and she said that none of them would sign. She says they're all afraid of Bart," he said.

"Did they give that as the reason?" Lettie asked, smoothing down the mountain of peanut butter on a slice of bread.

"No, they always gave some silly reason, like, 'I never sign papers,' or 'What good will it do? Once a thing like this bridge gets started, there's no stopping it.' " Jo spoke in the mincing tones he had heard.

"Why don't we go down and tell Will about your bad luck? I'll make a sandwich for him. I don't know why he hasn't come up to eat yet. He's usually hungry as a bear by this time." While Lettie worked she told Jo about the discovery of the green footprint.

"Curiouser and curiouser. I wish it hadn't vanished that way. We could have measured it and then compared its length with the shoes of suspects. Odd things are happening around here. Let's shoot down and tell Will about it," said Jo.

When they reached the boathouse, it was deserted. Will's tools were neatly placed on the overturned boat and there was a fresh white line of caulking cotton in a seam. The boy who had driven it in place was gone.

Jo and Lettie searched for Will along the shore. "Where *is* Will?" asked Lettie after they explored a small cove without finding him.

"Where *is* Will?" she repeated after they had searched in vain under the water-dripping, seaweed-hung walls of a tidal cave.

Her refrain was to be repeated many times before the day ended.

CHAPTER TWELVE

"WHERE IS WILL?"

When Jo and Lettie ran into the drugstore with the query, "Where is Will?" Ebbie answered.

"Will? Why, he's right down on the shore where he ought to be, working. Or leastways he was when I got called away. Whoops, that reminds me. I left my skiff high and dry. Mary Pete kind of scared me and I lit out in such a hurry I never moored the skiff off properly. Now the tide's gone down enough so I'll have to shove her a long way to the water. Do it now, I guess, 'fore it gets longer." Ebbie rose from the rocker with a groan.

"Take your time, Ebbie. I'll send Lettie with the bottle for Ivy Trafton," said Mary Pete.

When Ebbie had gone, she added, "I want you to take the order instead of Ebbie so you can go on to Bart's wharf and look for Will. You can see every bit of the harbor from the end of it."

Ebbie was soon back. "Where's my skiff at? You take and borry her, you kids?" he bellowed.

"Of course not," said Jo.

"Well, then, I guess wherever my skiff is, there'll you find Will," Ebbie answered.

Mary Pete said nothing, but the look of concern on her face increased. She gave Lettie the stoppered bottle for Mrs. Trafton. "Report right back, won't you?" she said.

Lettie and Jo posted off.

"While we're at it, let's ask Mrs. Trafton to sign our petition," she suggested.

Jo groaned. "I did, I did. She was the worst of the lot, a regular dragon. She only opened the door wide enough to show her face and that's not wide. She has a narrow, sharp face like a hatchet."

"Well, I'm going to ask her again. Maybe with this delivery to make, she'll let me in. Just opening the door a crack. Imagine!" Lettie's eyes blazed in a way that Jo admired. They almost shot sparks. Perhaps, after all, she could get the housekeeper to sign.

"Then I'll stick the stake with the red flag back in the ground before we go. The clothespin I put in to mark its place might get moved. I don't want to get Mary Pete in trouble with the engineers or anything," said Jo.

"Okay, but hustle. I'll sit on the wall and wait," Lettie answered.

Jo ran to the alder thicket and found the stake where he had tossed it. He had forgotten the jaunty feeling of this morning when he had set out with the stake across his shoulder. He circled the spot where he had left the clothespin marker. It had gone.

"For gosh sakes, hurry," Lettie called from the wall. "We don't have all day."

Like a hound on a scent Jo searched the lawn for the stake hole. When he found the grassless spot where he was sure it had been, he couldn't drive in the sapling. He ran to the woodshed for Ebbie's ax and wedge to enlarge the hole. With the ax's butt end he drove the triangular wedge into the ground.

After a few *tunk-tunks* he had a good piece of sod turned back. Then he was able to see why he had not succeeded in replacing the stake. A large stone had been in the way. He picked it out of the ground and tossed it aside. Something was beneath, a light-colored fragment. He picked it up and looked at it hastily. Lettie was chanting, "Hurry, will you, come on," and he must run off.

What he held in his hand was a fragment of broken dish, white with painted blue curlicues and a splotch of yellow.

"Funny," he said "looks mighty old." Then he slipped it into a dungaree pocket that was already knobby with seashells, pebbles, and his jackknife. He forgot it at once.

Lettie set the pace to Bart's house until they came near to its heavy frowning turrets. Then she slowed to a snail's gait.

"Why don't you come in with me after all, Jo? Two *might* have better luck than one." Her eyes were no longer flashing with indignation. In fact, she looked quite subdued at the thought of facing Mrs. Trafton.

Jo shook his head. He leaned against the far side of a great elm before the house.

Lettie advanced along the boardwalk slowly. At the back door she cleared her throat and knocked. Suddenly the door opened a crack.

"I'll take that medicine, thank you," said a dry voice. "And don't bother to unroll that paper you got under your arm there. I know what 'tis. I told Bart I thought Mary Pete was foolish taking in kids for the summer. We got enough troubles nowadays 'thout young ones knocking on doors with papers to sign."

Lettie's tongue stuck to the roof of her mouth, partly

from fear and partly from surprise at what she saw through the crack. Beyond the housekeeper was a three-colored cat stretched luxuriously on a doll's brass bedstead.

Lettie didn't wait for the door to close. In a daze she walked back to Jo. "It had sheets on it, that cat's bed," she said.

"I know, I saw it. She didn't sign, did she?" Jo answered as if he thought Lettie was taking his mind off her defeat.

"Well, we better hustle on to Bart's wharf. Will's been gone so long, I'm sort of worried," she answered.

They hurried on. The wind was blowing now. It flattened the grass and bent the supple hackmatack trees. The harbor was beaten to a steely flatness beneath it.

"Where *is* Will?" asked Lettie, shivering.

At Bart's wharf they found Sim in charge. He knew nothing about Will.

"If he was here, I didn't have no chance to see him. Been too tormented busy with Bart away to see much of anything," the boy told them. "Bart, he don't seem to think I mind being on duty twenty-four hours per day. With all these valuable snappers crated and ready to go I got to stick here. Bart called the truck to come for 'em and every lobster hijacker on the whole coast was probably listening in," Sim said importantly. "Can't take no chances," he added, patting the gun which he had lifted from the rack and laid across Bart's desk. Then he bought himself a coke from the red machine and turned up the volume of his small radio. Missing boys and skiffs were not important to him, that was plain.

Jo and Lettie left him to enjoy his own importance. They went out to the end of the wharf and looked off in all directions. There was not a skiff to be seen except for a few waiting at moorings for the return of lobster fishermen.

They hurried back to Mary Pete.

"Any news of Will?" she asked in a hopeful tone that showed she wasn't.

"No news," they answered dully.

"Let's go up to the widow's walk and take a look," Mary Pete suggested. "After all, it was built for such a purpose years ago."

Up through the house they went, single file, up the graceful curving staircase and then the scuffed attic steps. Behind one of the two great chimneys was a ladder-like staircase which the cousins had not noticed before. Mary Pete climbed it ahead of them. Halfway up she paused. "Notice how worn these treads are," she said. "They weren't made that way by folks coming up to admire the view. No, siree. What scooped out these hollows were the feet of wives coming up to look for menfolks who'd been two, three years away at sea. I imagine we feel now just about the way those ancestors of ours did."

Then she went on and raised a trap door above her head. The wind swept down into the attic. It sent the herb bunches spinning and the green carpet of herbs scuttling before it. If there had been the fresh imprint of a foot among them, it had been whirled away, Lettie thought.

When they stepped out onto the four-square platform on the roof, a tumult of wind attacked them. It lifted their hair, whistled up their sleeves, and made talking difficult.

"Up here on a good day you can see clear to Ballyhack and back," Mary Pete shouted, holding down her skirt.

They all hung on to the waist-high railing while they looked out. If they couldn't see "Ballyhack" they could see purple-blue Canadian hills and misty-blue American islands. A lobster boat, home from hauling, streaked across the water toward Bart's wharf.

"Del Snow, that is," Mary Pete shouted again, "in a hurry to get home." She knew the owner of every boat in the harbor.

Now the sun was moving down. Its brightness held no warmth. Clouds the color of blueberry stain moved across the sky. Nowhere on the harbor's somber surface was a small, leaky skiff with a boy at the oars.

Lettie shivered. "Guess I'll go down now," she said.

"So will we all," answered Mary Pete.

Not long after they reached the warm kitchen, Ebbie burst in upon them. He carried a battered oar. "This here's mine!" he announced. "Del Snow picked her up just now, floating off the end of Eden. He thought by the look of her she was mine so he brought her in. I was down to the shore when he came."

For a moment no one spoke. They all knew what the finding of that oar could mean.

"Del gave me the loan of his skiff. I'm going out and take a look-see along the island. Probably my skiff's hung up somewhere out there. Maybe Will took her out to Smuggler's Cove and lost the oars and now he can't row back. I feel kind of responsible, don't you know, because I invited him to go out there in the first place. Maybe he thought he'd go out alone and investigate the Cove—"

Ebbie's words slowed and finally trailed off as if his hopes of finding Will were running out as he spoke.

"How about taking me along?" asked Jo.

"And me?" asked Lettie.

"Come along, the both of you. Ample room in that skiff o' Del's. You come, too, Mary Pete."

"No," she answered. "I'm going to tend shop and ring up the Coast Guard so they will have an eye out for Will. Now bundle up warm, you two. It'll be mighty cold out there on the water before you're through."

It was mighty cold, they found, long before they reached the island. They huddled into their jackets and tried not to shiver. Ebbie rowed the skiff along the Eden shore and explored every nook and guzzle hole. The island no doubt was a lovely spot on a sunny day. This afternoon, with the tide well down and dark brown rockweed hanging from the ledges, it was downright gloomy.

"This Smuggler's Cove we're going into now is where one of my grandfathers did a bit of smuggling," Ebbie told them as they passed between two arms of ledge that almost met. "He didn't make a living of it, you understand, just wool for his own use, 'twas. I guess everybody in them days did a bit to save paying duty. Later, in Prohibition days, there was a pile of rum came in here from Canada. Cases of the stuff set right on that shore under them very trees." Ebbie pointed out the spot. "Of course the fellers that brought 'em in all got caught sooner or later and went to federal prison for a year and a day. Since then it's been calm and peaceful here. And now there's Bart proposing to stir things up again with this bridge."

Ebbie rowed into the center of the cove. There was no skiff along the curve of shingle beach. The spirits of the searchers were as dark as the wall of giant spruce trees beyond the rocks.

They finished the circuit of the island. Lettie and Jo had little hope now of finding Ebbie's skiff. A few skiffs were beached but Ebbie soon identified them as belonging to others. The small rise of hope was quenched.

On their return Mary Pete's greeting was cheerful. "I've called the Coast Guard station. They're sending out a motor surfboat to look for Will. And Del Snow rang up. He's got a a gang rounded up and just as soon as they've had a bite to eat the men are going out again in their boats for a search."

Mary Pete didn't need to ask them the result of theirs. Three discouraged faces told her as soon as they came into the kitchen.

"We'll have a bite ourselves now you're back. Corned

100

beef, potatoes boiled in their jackets, and goose-grass greens. How does that sound?" Mary Pete drained the vegetables as she talked. A cloud of steam fogged the windows. "Stay, Ebbie. Plenty to eat here for all hands and the cook."

They sat at the table but only Mary Pete ate much. No doubt she did so to set a good example.

"I guess I'll save my goose-grass greens and stuff till tomorrow, if it's okay by you, Mary Pete," Lettie said after a polite struggle with her supper. "Somehow I feel the way I did at the cracker race when Bart drove in with his old picture of the bridge. I think about Will and my throat shuts up. I'm sorry."

The others too gave up the attempt to eat.

Mary Pete said, "I'm going into the shop now. I can stick near the phone while I work on a couple of orders. You folks keep a lookout here."

As if we could do anything else, thought the cousins. They saw five lobster boats set out to search for Will, then they huddled in the dark by the kitchen window to wait for their return. The setting sun sent a pink afterglow over the harbor and gradually it turned dark. Straining their eyes and ears, the two stared into the night.

After a long time two moving lights in the distance became two boats as they neared the moorings. The wind drowned out the sound of the motors. Later, one at a time, three more came in as silently.

"Let's go tell Mary Pete the boats are all in," said Jo.

Lettie picked up the flashlight from the shelf and snapped it on. They went out into the windy night.

"The men are all back, Mary Pete," they called as they went into the shop.

"We'll probably have a ring from them any minute now. Perhaps we'll be seeing our Will in jig time."

Fifteen minutes dragged by like five hours and the phone

did not ring. Then three rings came, and Mary Pete picked up the receiver.

"No luck at all," came the voice of a tired man, "we did our best for you but we didn't see a thing. Any word from the fellows at the Coast Guard?"

"Not a word," said Mary Pete in a flat voice. "I can't say thanks enough to you all for going out, Del Snow. Go to bed now and get your sleep. Good night."

She hung up, then turned to the others. "That's it for tonight, I'm afraid. You two skip to bed. Ebbie's going to keep me company. The minute we get news, we'll wake you up."

Much as they wanted to stay here, they obeyed. They settled down on their beds without undressing to be ready for Mary Pete's call. The old house, they found, was too full of odd creaks and groans for sleep on this windy night. Their thoughts were even more disturbed. Lettie remembered suddenly the footprint in the attic with its outline of green herbs, the switching about of the tags, the disappearance from the kitchen shelf of the old copybook. Whoever had done these things might still be hiding somewhere in this rambling house. Her mind was spinning in this circle when she heard a strange new sound. A wailing roar, it was.

She sat bolt upright. "You awake, Jo?" she called.

"What do you expect?" was his cross answer.

"What's a banshee?" Lettie asked.

"You know as well as I do," was his even crosser reply.

And so she did. A banshee was a creature that wailed out of darkness to tell of a tragic event or death. Who would believe in such a creature nowadays, she asked herself, while she thought, maybe I'm hearing one! The dancing shadows of the candle on her bureau and the mournful sounds of the old house were affecting her strangely.

"Jo," she called again, "I'm going to the shop. That noise out there *is* like a banshee. Can't you hear it?"

"So am I. No sense just lying here wide-awake," he answered.

Thy went downstairs together within the small circle of light from Lettie's candle. In the kitchen Jo snapped on the flashlight. Its strong beam drove old-fashioned thoughts of banshees and such from their minds. That is until they opened the door and heard from over the water that anguished roar. They ran to the shop.

CHAPTER THIRTEEN

WILL MAKES UP HIS MIND

Will, shut in the locker aboard the *Elmira,* assured himself that he wasn't frightened, no, not in the least. For some reason his own knees disagreed with him and shook in the darkness in a way that surprised him. He could, they seemed to remind him, be in danger. If Black Bart or Harry discovered him, they could lock the door and leave him to suffocate.

Will had ample time for wondering as he lay here in the dark. Birds of a feather flocked together. If Harry were like Bart he was a very black crow indeed, and Will didn't like the thought of being at his mercy.

A moment came when the cabin was empty. Will decided he must stretch a bit and breathe deeply while the men were on deck. Later he wouldn't dare to do either. The very thought made his throat tickle with the desire to cough.

He put his hands over his head as far as they could go. He wiggled his fingers. One hand touched an object that was not wooden like the mummy-shaped locker that encased him. It was cold and metallic. He explored it with both hands. Even blind as a bat, he knew what it was. It was a revolver!

Now the coldness meeting his fingertips on touching it tingled along his spine. Bart's friend *was* a very bad crow. This proved it. No man on honest business would carry a gun slid like this one into a casing of bent nails.

Why, oh, why, didn't I have the sense to stay on shore? I would be safely stuffing cotton in a crack and getting the skiff ready. Then his adventurous spirit rose. I'm glad I'm here, he thought. I'm in the best spot to make an important discovery. What's more, he thought somewhat wryly, here I am cruising on the *Elmira*. What more could I want?

Soon darkness and warmth made him doze off.

When he woke, the throb of the engine and the creak of boards under strain had gone. In the quietness he could hear a steady *slap-slap* of water against the sides. They were no longer under way.

He noticed another difference, too. Fumes of cooking spaghetti sauce were drifting into the locker. Soon it was full of them, and his nose and throat as well. As for his stomach, that was affected, too. Was he about to be seasick, he wondered.

He heard the rattle of cutlery, a slam of plates, a scraping of pots. In a short time the murmur of contented talk told Will that the meal was being enjoyed. Never, never could he look at the greasy, slippery stuff again. How could he ever have liked spaghetti?

I am not going to be sick, I can't be sick, I just am not, he told himself stoutly. He put one hand firmly across his mouth, the other on his stomach to tell them he was master.

"Here, Harry, have some more grated cheese. Got enough to drown in, you might say. Take a lot," Bart urged his friend.

Will clenched his teeth in the darkness. Can I stick it out? I've got to have fresh air soon. What shall I do if they turn in for the night without leaving the cabin? He had no idea what time it was. The only clue he had was a thin line of electric light in the crack of the door.

This meal going on in the cabin must be the longest ever eaten, Will thought. Finally, with the sound of piling plates and cutlery, he knew it had ended.

"Your Mrs. Trafton is sure a good spaghetti cook," said Harry.

If only they would stop talking about the food, thought Will.

After a time the men went up on deck.

Cautiously, gingerly, Will moved his arms up and back and pushed open the locker door. He slid on his back until his head was outside and resting on the bunk. Ah, this air was better, although the cabin was heavy with cooking odors. I must get to the nearest porthole and get it open, if I do get caught, he thought.

He slid on his back until his head touched a paper bagful of supplies. He pushed it to one side. To his ears the crackle of paper sounded like a Christmas bough bursting into flame. No move from the men on deck. Will held his breath and inched to the porthole. He turned the threaded screw that held it shut. He pushed the round glass port until there was an opening wide enough for his face. Then he drew in great lungfuls of fresh salt air as if he had never before had this pleasure.

The full moon, rising pink, popped up over the horizon. How odd to see the face of a friend so familiar from this strange spot.

Quickly and silently he closed the port. Then he lay down once more and slid back into his hole, more like a snake than a rabbit this time. Carefully he pulled the locker door after him until the same necessary crack was left.

He was just in time. One of the men, he never knew which, came down into the cabin. The lighthearted feet tapped down and then up and out. Phew, that had been a close call!

Now that he had breathed fresh air, Will felt better. He dozed.

He woke with a start. The *squawk-crackle-phst-whee* of a radio being tuned in filled the air.

"Staticky tonight, ain't it?" said Harry. "Guess I'll keep her on just the same so's we can get the weather. I want to know if it's a good idea to lie here tonight. It's kind of exposed if the wind swings 'round."

The static gave way to words. ". . . tonight the Coast Guard personnel are out in full force in eastern coastal waters," came a voice, "seeking a young boy missing and presumed drowned. Uncle Sam's Coast Guard is being joined in this search by most of the lobster fishing fleet from the village of Surprise Harbor where young Will Dennis, thirteen, is visiting his cousin, Miss Mary P. Tibbetts. Now for the marine interests, the weather . . ."

A loud snap ended the broadcast.

"Say, fellow, what's the idea, turning her off? I want to get my weather," Harry protested.

"We're going straight back to Surprise Harbor, that's the idea. That boy that's missing is the cousin of a friend of mine. If I can help her find him, I will."

Was this Black Bart speaking? Will could hardly trust his ears.

"That's what you think," said Harry. "I happen to have other plans for my boat. The hook's coming up all right, but we're heading on down East. I'm not going to hang around and have Uncle Sam's Coast Guard come poking its nose aboard of *my* craft."

"What you got against the Coast Guard, or is it they got something against you?" Bart asked.

"You might say we don't see eye to eye on certain matters. I'm just not having them stop my boat and ask questions, and that's flat, see? I'm heading for Canada as fast as I can. What's more, I'm going to have that weather broadcast back on."

The words "Eastport to Block Island" suddenly jumped out. As suddenly the broadcast was shut off.

"You're looking for trouble, fellow, when you do a thing like that!" Harry's voice was even sharper than the metallic scratching of the broadcaster's voice.

"Trouble or not, you're taking me back to Surprise," said Bart.

"I'm taking *you!* Listen, my friend, I'm captain here. I don't take no one but me where I want to go." A steely edge in Harry's tones set Will's knees to wobbling again.

"Mighty afraid of that Coast Guard, aren't you?" Bart taunted.

"Call it I'm being careful, if you like," Harry answered. "I don't know why you should be so all-fired surprised that I want to stay clear of them Coast Guard fellows. I can't hardly believe you think I'm a lobster dealer pure and simple. If you had the wits, you'd ought to know I got other fish to fry. I suppose you thought I was helping you build a good lobster pound and all as a charity case, eh? You and your bridge!" He paused as if choked by scorn. "Bridge to nowhere is what I call it. It'll be that for sure if you don't have me to back you. Without me, it'll be nothing."

Will wanted to cover his ears and at the same to listen hard. The more he learned, the less safe he felt. Somehow he couldn't quite believe that Black Bart was Mary Pete's friend.

Suddenly words gave way to blows. Will heard thuds and bangs as the two men struggled. They bumped against the fittings and whacked against the bunks. Will slid down as far into the locker as he could and curled up small. He hoped he wouldn't be seen if the locker door flew open.

"We're going back!" Bart spoke in a strained voice.

"We're going where I say!" was Harry's answer.

The two remarks were hurled like knives. Soon a plate crashed to the deck, a tin can thudded and rolled. The sounds of struggle were coming nearer to Will's locker.

It's the gun that Harry is after! He's trying to get here to grab it. And when he does it will be bad for Bart and bad for me.

Then suddenly Will thought, *but I'm the one that has the gun. All I have to do is grab the gun, shove open the door, and spring out. Then I'd say, "Put them up." I could do it.*

He reached up to discover how the gun was fastened to the locker overhead. One, two, three nails, he counted. There was none on the side toward the locker door. Harry had fastened it thus to be slid out in a hurry. Will tried to move the gun. It came free easily in his hands.

With the revolver in his hand he felt a sudden panic. If it were loaded, it might go off suddenly. Then nothing would be gained and a great deal lost. Harry, warned, could seize the gun and Bart and Will both would be out of luck. Or worse. But Will didn't want to think about that.

While Will, undecided, held the gun, the radio was snapped on.

"Lullaby and good-night, with roses bedight—"

Although the weather report was over, Harry had won a victory in turning on his radio.

"Bright angels around my baby shall stand—" Words meant to soothe burst out in a crackling roar.

Surely Bart would end this ghastly noise if he could. He must be losing the struggle.

Then a thought flashed into Will's mind like a rocket

across a night sky. *This noise is what I need. Harry can't hear me if I move out now.* He held the gun lightly while he rolled over onto his stomach and pushed open the locker door. For a moment the brightness in the room blinded him. When his eyes grew used to the light he saw Harry and Bart struggling together. Bart's back was toward him. Harry faced the locker but his mouth was open, his eyes squeezed tight shut as he struggled.

Neither man saw Will. He slid out onto the bunk, whipped out his legs, and stood up. His knees were wobbly, his mouth dry.

He tried to say in a ringing voice, "Put them up." Instead, the words "Here I am, Bart," came out weakly, almost a cry for help.

However, he stood his ground.

Harry let Bart go. He swung about swiftly. Both men lunged at Will, or was it at the gun? Will's words may have been weak but his hold on the gun was firm. He pointed it toward Harry.

CHAPTER FOURTEEN

"OLD ROARER"

When Jo and Lettie ran from the house and burst into the shop that night, they found their cousin still at work.

"Don't you hear it, too?" Lettie asked her.

"Hear what?" asked Mary Pete as calmly as if she were asked this question at midnight every day of the week.

"Hear what?" asked Ebbie, straightening up in his rocking chair. He had been dozing with his mouth open and his neck bent like a broken doll's. "I weren't asleep, just resting my eyes, don't you know."

Mary Pete laid down the fat pottery pestle with which she had been grinding some substance in a white mortar. "What with my work noises and Ebbie's snores, I haven't heard your noises, I guess."

"Listen, now listen!" Lettie commanded, and held up one finger for attention. No one spoke. Soon the banshee sound, a roar with an undertone of wailing anguish, rose into the air.

"You mean that?" asked Ebbie. "Why, that's nothing

but the whirlpool out there. Didn't no one tell you about her?"

Both Jo and Lettie solemnly shook their heads.

Ebbie laughed. "I suppose if you didn't know, 'twould kind of put you off a bit. Yes, it's the whirlpool. 'Old Roarer,' we call it when it gets talking that way. Always speaks up so, like a lion roaring, when the tide's flowing in extra high on account of the full moon."

He tipped back in his chair to look out. "And, by jiminy, there's the moon now. Wind's blown away the clouds and she's a-rising full. Just look at her. Don't she have the air of knowing all the answers with that expression on her face?"

Old Roarer's bloodcurdling wail came again.

When the sound died away, Mary Pete announced in a flat voice, "I called your folks, Lettie, to let them know that Will is missing. I thought I should. It was the hardest thing I ever did but I knew that they would never forgive me if I didn't."

"Are they going to come?" asked Lettie.

"Yes, they hope to set out by sunrise. They said they approved what I'd done, my calling the Coast Guard and letting the lobster boats go out to look for Will, and they're coming."

"Oh," said Lettie, and felt that suddenly Will's disappearance seemed more awful than before. Notifying her family made it somehow official.

"As for me," Mary Pete went on, "I can never forgive myself if anything has happened to Will. I never dreamed when I wrote my invitations for the old house's last summer that a thing like this might happen. That shows you how little imagination I've got. Oh, dear."

"It's really not in the least your fault, Mary Pete. If Will

took it into his head to, well, it's his own—" A lump in her throat ended Lettie's attempt to cheer her cousin.

"How about letting us stay in the shop with you and Ebbie?" asked Jo. "We'll never in this world go to sleep, that's for sure."

"Why, okay," Mary Pete answered. "If you do get to feeling drowsy, you can help yourself to Ebbie's couch. He's able to sleep in a chair."

"Don't know why you think I was sleeping; I was listening in case the Coast Guard motor surfboat came in. That's why I was so quiet," Ebbie protested.

"You weren't talking much," Mary Pete agreed with a slight smile, "but you were hardly what I'd call quiet, either. Hark, now, does anyone hear a boat coming in?"

They all listened, but Old Roarer raising his voice once again was all they heard.

They waited. The moon, mysterious as ever, rose high. After a time the whirlpool ceased its sounds of anguish. Jo jigged up and down on to couch. Ebbie rocked, his eyes on the harbor. Lettie wandered through the shop, glad that Mary Pete had installed electric lights here so that she could read the names on the crystal jars. Tonight, however, not even their magic succeeded in taking her thoughts off Will. *Ginseng root, Vermont; star anise seeds, China; dragon's blood, China*— There was no use. She could see nothing but her brother's face. *Cinnamon, Ceylon*, didn't say the Orient to her any more. It only reminded her how much Will liked cinnamon toast. With her brother missing, Lettie felt more and more only half a person.

Jo's thoughts were equally unchangeable. He saw Will's eager face as he drew one of the long slips from Lettie's hand this morning. If he had drawn the short piece, he might be asleep in bed now.

114

Lettie gave up her study of the jars and joined Jo on the couch.

Suddenly Mary Pete burst out, "Oh, I do wish Bart were here and not cruising with his fancy friend. I need his help."

Lettie and Jo exchanged glances. Whatever could this startling remark mean, wanting Black Bart, of all people, to be here now? They didn't ask because their cousin had made her admission as if she were alone.

A funny quirk that was almost a smile appeared at the corners of Ebbie's lips. "I thought the last few years you calculated you were doing better when he weren't around. What in the world good could he do?"

"I really don't know what he or anyone else could do right now," Mary Pete admitted. "As for me, I guess my brain is getting addled, to even think he could help."

Then, "Harkee," said Ebbie, one forefinger raised.

They listened. A boat was coming in.

"The Coast Guard?" asked Jo as he and Lettie ran to the window.

"Nope, only a lobster smack, looks like, bound for Bart's. Might have known," said Ebbie.

The waiting went on.

CHAPTER FIFTEEN

WILL AND BART JOIN FORCES

Although Will's "Here I am, Bart," was quavery, the two men struggling in the *Elmira*'s cabin heard it. Even with the radio blaring, "Lullaby and good-night, with roses bedight," for the third time, Will made himself heard.

Instantly Harry let go Bart's shoulders. Bart, whose back had been toward Will, whirled about. Both the men lunged at him.

"That gun's not loaded. You might as well put it down," Harry said harshly.

Just the same, Will clung to it and kept it pointed. Loaded or not, both Harry and Bart wanted it, that was plain. They grabbed for it. Will, gun held high, jumped up onto the nearer bunk and ran aft along the slippery mattress.

Now the two men struggled together again, this time to reach Will.

"That's my gun, boy, give it here!" Harry bellowed. "What's more I'm captain of this boat."

With the hand that wasn't holding the gun Will reached down and snapped off the radio. The nerve-shattering song ended in a squawk. In the silence Will heard the men panting as they grappled.

Suddenly Will found the courage to call out as he had meant to at first, "Put up your hands, Mr. Harry, or I'll shoot." His voice was firm and strong this time.

This did it. Harry proved that the gun, as Will suspected, was loaded. Up went his hands.

Will's knees began a little dance all by themselves. With this quick success, Will was more frightened than ever.

"Keep them up," he said less firmly.

Bart swung at Harry. Down he fell with such a whack of his head against a bunk that Will was almost sorry for him. While Harry lay sprawled and slightly dazed, Bart was able to jump him.

"Guess you can safely put down that gun now," Bart said as he straddled Harry's chest. "Hustle up on deck. Get me that line that's coiled near the wheel. Reach the knife out of my pants pocket. Cut the line and bring it here. Fast!"

Will laid down the gun thankfully in a far corner. Then he carried out Bart's orders. Soon the *Elmira*'s captain was trussed like a Christmas bird ready for the oven. While the work went on Harry told Bart what he thought of him. If Bart heard himself being described as the scum of the earth, he gave no sign.

He did hear Harry when he said, "I sure feel lousy. That spaghetti sauce of yours."

"You may feel lousier before the night's over," Bart answered. "We're taking a little trip to the Coast Guard station on our way home. I may be a jackass up to a certain point, Harry, but you didn't think I hadn't guessed what you were up to, did you? For a long time I've been sure that you wanted more out of me than a market for your illegal lobsters. No man would go to all the pains you take without a lot at stake. You thought when you had me mixed up with you and those lobsters, you could blackmail me into running in other stuff, something with a high duty on it maybe, tucked in among your lobsters, didn't you?"

"If you're so smart, why do you ask me that? Find out for yourself," said Harry. He shut his eyes as if he wanted to think about something else.

Bart had no more conversation with him. He checked the knots he had tied in lashing Harry. Then he told him, "Don't you worry about harm coming to your boat. I know all these waters like the back of my hand. With my crew here I'll take good care of your *Elmira,* Harry. She's much too good a boat for you."

The *Elmira's* captain was not provoked to answer, even by the sarcasm in his speech.

Bart and Will went up on deck. By this time Will had almost forgotten his membership in the "Down-with-Black-Bart Society." Working with Bart seemed a natural thing to be doing.

Bart shut the cabin door after them and shot the bolt. "There, that ought to hold him for a bit," Bart said.

"He certainly gave up easily," Will remarked in a worried tone.

"Oh, I know his kind," Bart answered. "He's all talk, up to a certain point. Then, p-h-h-t, he collapses like a burst balloon at a birthday party. Besides, don't forget we have this." He patted his pocket.

Will had forgotten the gun in spite of his fear of it. "Have you put its safety on?"

Bart nodded. He continued his talk about Harry. "Yes,

he's the same kind of fellow his father was before him. I've always heard tales about Harry Senior in the days he was running rum from Canada and the French Islands—"

Bart's talk was punctuated with preparations for getting the yawl under way. We had the motor running as he said, "Yes, sir, Harry Senior was a great hand to come into Surprise with a wad of bills would choke a horse. He'd show it 'round and then announce there was a lot of cases of rum on such-and-such an island. Anyone wanted to make good use of his spare time and his boat, why, all he had to do was row out there and boat those cases in. *And* see that a certain truck connected with them on the first moonless night."

Now the *Elmira*'s anchor was up and chocked on deck.

"Did many of the Surprise people bring in the rum?"

"Not one, as far as I know," Bart answered. "He had to go somewhere else." Now they were moving from the small cove where Harry had anchored. The peaked trees on shore showed darker than the sky. "Some were tempted to share that roll of Harry Senior's. Money was mighty scarce in those days. Tempted or not, the folks all got a boot out of one thing that happened to the rumrunner. He was getting too big for his britches and doing pretty well in spite of a few setbacks, such as losing a load or two to revenue agents. He had it in for one agent in particular who had been the cause of his losses. Cocky as all get out, he called this man on the phone and taunted him, told him he had put a load of stuff on a Canadian island called the Devil's Pulpit. He dared him to go out and take it off. Of course he knew the man didn't have the legal right because it was not in American territory. He didn't count on what the agent would do, however, and that was to call the Canadian police. They zoomed out and took the whole load. It served Harry Senior right, I'd say. Anyhow, his son is a chip off the old block; he's after a fast buck and honesty doesn't enter in."

Now the *Elmira* was purring along in open water. Will's enjoyment of this part of his cruise made up for the earlier fear and discomfort. The moon was well up. Their wake was edged with a curl of gold. As for the air, Will couldn't seem to get his fill of this wonderful freshness.

"Gorry, it sure is a fine night," said Bart. He grinned at Will and he replied by laughing. Bart was enjoying this adventure as much as he, that was plain. It sent a burst of happiness through him to think that he and Bart were really on the same side.

"The moon's so bright tonight you can scarcely see the Milkmaid's Path up there," said Bart, pointing to the Milky Way.

On the outer shore the lighthouses were carrying on their nightly conversations. One tower swung an arm of light, a second stared with a steady eye, a third winked intermittently. Back home poor Jo and Lettie would be tucked up asleep and missing all the magnificence of this night.

"Do you suppose when we get to the Coast Guard station they'd let me send word to Mary Pete not to worry and that I'll soon be home?" Will asked.

Bart nodded. "If you didn't let her know, I would," he said.

A faint pink stirred in the eastern sky as the *Elmira* nosed into the Ragged Island cove where the Coast Guard had its station. By this time Will and Bart were fast friends. Even so, there were still a good many things to be explained. As with most grownups, certain questions would have to remain unasked. Bart would have to say why he had persisted in his plan for the bridge long after he mistrusted Harry's intentions.

In the cove they saw the white shape of a surfboat

moored off the boathouse slip. Near it a white buoy marked
an empty mooring. Somewhat paled by the approach of
dawn, lights burned outside the boathouse and in the yard
of the station. The dark outline of a man on watch stood
out in a lighted window.

"Kind of them to have an empty mooring ready for us,
wasn't it?" asked Bart, grinning. "I have a hunch the boat
that usually rides there is out looking for a certain Will
Dennis, thirteen. They'll be some surprised to have you
show up on your own. Grab the boathook, will you, and
let's see how good you are at picking up a mooring."

Will ran forward with the hook. He was determined to
get the mooring on his first try. They moved up to it with
the bow wave gurgling its song. Will lunged out with the
boathook and, clunk, the buoy was banging the side on its
way up. He spoke a quiet "Hurrah!" for his own ears.

They were about to step down into the skiff trailing
astern when Bart said, "I wonder if we should take a look
at our prisoner before we go ashore. He ought to be safe
for a month of Sundays. I used about every knot in the
book on him." He put his ear to the crack in the cabin
door. "Not a sound."

They rowed to the boathouse slip. Before they reached
the station the door opened. "Hi, friends, come on in. It's
not often we have callers at this hour. What's on your
minds?" asked a young Coast Guardsman.

"For one thing, here's your missing boy from Surprise,"
said Bart.

"The boys are still out looking for him. I'll tell them to
call it off," said the Coast Guardsman.

"Oh, please, could you call my cousin, too? She's probably kind of upset by this," said Will.

"Come in, come in. I'm on radio guard and I was just
about to have a mug-up. How about joining me?" As he

spoke, the young man ushered them in. Then he filled three mugs with steaming coffee.

"This'll go good," said Bart as he took his cup. "We had sort of a rough time aboard." He blew across the surface of the liquid before he tried it.

"That so?" said the young man. "By the way, I'm Seaman Moore. They call me Vint." He waited for Bart's story.

It was delayed. The sound of a starting motor made them look out toward the cove. On the deck of the *Elmira* was a dark shape. It was Harry, freed from his bonds.

In a moment the yawl would be gone, unless the watchers could prevent it.

CHAPTER SIXTEEN

HARD AGROUND

"Well, I'll be!" said Bart. "Houdini himself. How in time did he untie those knots? Maybe I should put a scare in him with this."

He drew Harry's gun from his pocket and fired into the air above the yawl. The effect of the shot, however, was not to stop Harry. It sent him scrambling and crouching down into the cockpit. Soon the *Elmira* was speeding away.

The watchers on shore stood motionless in surprise. The mainmast merged with the tall spruces on the point.

"Now he won't stop nor draw breath until he gets to Canada. As for me, I ought to have my head examined," said Bart. He groaned.

Vint cocked his head and listened. "Yup, I thought so. There's a motor coming in, too. Bet you a cookie it's our motor lifeboat with the boys back from hunting for this one. Maybe if we meet her at the mooring we'll stand a chance of catching up with your friend before he reaches Canada. I'll get someone to take radio guard and away we'll go."

Bart and Will hurried to the boathouse and Vint soon overtook them wearing a warm pea jacket over his blue shirt. The *Elmira*'s skiff was soon on its way to meet the newcomers.

Skiff and lifeboat met at the mooring, or, rather, where the mooring buoy had been. When he had heard the shot, Harry in his haste to take off had cut the line. The buoy was bobbing free toward shore.

"Blast that fellow's hide," said Vint. "Look what he's done. Now someone's got to go down in that cold water and pick up the mooring chain that he's cut off. Likely it'll be me. I once made the mistake of saying I liked skin diving. Since then, if there's any underwater salvage going on, I'm the one that gets tapped for it."

It didn't take Vint long to tell the men in the lifeboat what they wanted. Soon the three in the skiff were aboard and they were off in pursuit of the *Elmira*.

"We'll catch up with the fellow," said the sailor at the wheel. "We'll get him if we have to go to the border."

The surfboat leaped forward. The throb of the diesel engine was so powerful that it was almost visible, like heat waves shimmering above a stove.

To Canada, Will thought. This is really a break. I will be the first of us three to get there.

Harry disappointed him in not heading for Canada. At first he appeared to make for Puffin Island Lighthouse across the border. Then realizing he was pursued, he swung the *Elmira* toward the mainland. The Coast Guard followed suit.

Before the game of tag had lasted very long, Bart exclaimed in disgust, "Harry's a fool. He's going to run her aground."

"Thinks more of his skin than his boat, I'll warrant," answered the man at the wheel.

"I wouldn't give much for his skin if he lands there on Spruce Point where he's headed," said Bart. "It's every bit as wild as when the Indians owned it. As for mosquitoes, phew! Misery Heath, which he'll have to cross if he intends to get inland, raises the biggest and best I ever met. He'll wish he'd stayed on his comfortable boat, or I miss my guess. He'll be a mass of mosquito bites and briar scratches."

If the *Elmira* made a loud crash when she struck, her pursuers were too far astern to hear. When they slowed for a look, the silent yawl was wedged fast between two rockweed-hung ledges. They held her upright and there she rested, still beautiful and dignified and, as far as they could see, unscathed.

"She's probably strained herself good," Bart announced. Then he halloed, "Hey, Harry."

There was no answer. The spruce forest came so far down on the ledges here that branches were tangled in the yawl's bowsprit. Harry could easily have leaped ashore.

"Well, fellows," said the chief, "no point that I can see in our taking off after him if the terrain is as bad as we've heard. We'd better board her and have a look around. Maybe there's some evidence of this Harry's stock in trade."

The lifeboat was moored off at a safe distance and Bart ferried them in, two at a time, in the *Elmira's* skiff.

"She's certainly wedged in good," said Vint. He and Will were the first two arrivals. They clambered up the weed-hung ledges, clinging to handfuls of the rubbery fronds when the incline was steep. Overhead a gull fanned past. It croaked in an amazed tone, as if to say, "What's this, more humans on Spruce Point?"

Although they felt fairly sure that Harry had abandoned ship, they climbed aboard the *Elmira* with extreme caution.

Will warned Vint that Harry was a scrapper. Already they had seen the smashed companionway door from the height which they had needed to climb to get onto the yawl.

"Oh-ho," said Vint, fingering the splintered door panels, "your friend sure did a job here. Clobbered up his door good, he did, when he broke out of there."

They went down into the cabin. Beneath the table lay the cut line with which Bart had trussed Harry. From this tangle gleamed the blade of a bread knife. Somehow Harry had inched himself along and maneuvered until his hands met the knife.

As the Coast Guardsmen arrived they were full of cheer and of ideas for a search.

"First place to look is the least likely," said one.

The others tapped and thumped and looked wise.

Will had no theory about looking. His own search was rather aimless. He looked in cupboards and lifted up and put down again all sorts of gear. What should he be expecting to find—would it be diamonds or drugs or stolen paintings?

In due course he opened the mummy-shaped cupboard where he had spent so many hours. He looked in and was not surprised to find it empty. He turned to its mate across the aisle. This was crammed as before with all manner of sea gear—life jackets, lines, a foghorn. Will peered in hoping for a surprise of some sort and it seemed a longer compartment than the other.

"Vint," he said to the sailor, "these two cupboards ought to be exactly the same shape, shouldn't they? They aren't. This one looks a good bit longer."

"That so," said Vint. "Well, the quickest way to settle that is measure them both."

He picked up a mop from a corner and rammed its handle into the crowded cupboard. The handle disappeared, the gray cotton mop went out of sight, and Vint's arm followed it, almost to his shoulder.

"That's it for length here. Now we measure its twin." Vint ran the mop handle into Will's hiding place and even before the gray mop went out of sight, the mop handle struck the back with a thud.

"You're right, kid, this one is shorter by a good bit. I'm going in there and find out why." He took a jackknife from his pocket and opened the largest blade. Then, headfirst, in he went with the knife in one hand. The others crowded close to watch. Only the soles of Vint's feet were visible. They rocked from side to side as he attacked the back of the locker.

Soon the feet came traveling out, followed by legs. Then a triumphant Vint was out among them. He waved a package wrapped in tissue paper. He laid it on the table and, with what seemed to Will very slow motion, unrolled it.

There lay a dozen shining tablespoons, their bowls nested. Vint picked up a spoon and turned it over on his palm. On its back, where the flat handle narrowed toward the bowl, were the letters, *HOLLAND.* "Well, don't that beat all? The whole place in there is solid with the stuff, jampacked. They must have put all the packages in with a shoehorn."

"Well, sir," said the chief, "I guess that proves what we want to know. This Dutch stainless steel has got pretty high duty on it. 'Twould really pay a fellow to run in a load. Now when the tide floats this craft we'll take her in to the Customs men."

"What happens then?" asked Will. He didn't want an ignoble end for the *Elmira.* Two days ago he had seen a sardine carrier plowing up the bay to the fish factory. The boat lacked a mast but her bow still held the bowsprit useless since her bygone days as a yacht.

"Then," said the chief, "the Customs men will use the evidence of these smuggled goods. They'll declare her forfeit and put her up for sale. She'll be advertised in the paper for several weeks. That way, the interested parties will know so they can bid on her."

A wild hope sprang up in Will's heart. "How long, how long will they keep her first?" he asked.

The chief laughed as though he read Will's thoughts. "Not until you get rich enough to buy her, I guess, but a while. Don't know the law on it exactly."

Will's hope died as quickly as it had been born. He'd never have time to earn money for the *Elmira*.

Bart had a twinkle in his eyes that was almost a conspirator's. All he said, however, was, "Now how are we going to get ourselves back to Surprise? Without the *Elmira*, we'll have to go in her skiff."

"Don't worry. We'll undertake to get you two home. Guess we'd better leave you here, Vint, till she floats free. Our smuggler just might take it into his head to come back and try to salvage his boat. The rest of us'll go to the station and fill up our tanks. We got mighty low on diesel oil looking for that poor kid that was drowned." The chief gave Will a gentle slap on the back. "I don't think we left a square inch of water unchurned looking for you."

Will envied Vint this chance to stay and explore for more smuggled goods.

At Ragged Island the chief went ashore. As he said goodby he added, "I'll let the folks at Surprise know first thing you're safe and sound and on the way home. Young fellow, we'll keep you posted on the *Elmira*. If anything more turns up on her, we'll let you know."

With its tank full the motor lifeboat raced toward Surprise. Soon the sun was rising. Its golden light bathed both white boats and gulls overhead. It made bright rainbows in the wings of foam that they swept to each side.

"This is really traveling," said Will. He and Bart stood by the man at the wheel. "I never thought we'd be taking a trip like this together."

Bart grinned. "Nor did I, any kind of trip, with Mary Pete to advise you against keeping bad company like me."

This might be the moment to ask some questions of Bart —about the bridge, about his teaming up with a smuggler like Harry. These matters had plagued Will with wonders and doubts for a long time. He opened his mouth to make a start and as quickly closed it. After all, there were a few questions that Bart could ask, too. "What were you doing on the *Elmira* so secret that you had to climb in a cupboard?" was one.

No, it was best to wait until he talked with Jo and Lettie. They were still members of the "Down-with-Black-Bart Society."

CHAPTER SEVENTEEN

HOMECOMING AND HIJACKERS

From Mary Pete's shop the weary watchers saw the bright disc of the sun pop up over Eden Island. Its light gilded the peaked spruce tops and for a moment turned a crow perched upon one into a shining weathercock.

The bird flapped off. Soon the telephone rang, three rings. They all jumped up to answer but Lettie was first to reach the instrument.

"Hello. Yes, right here. He is! They are! Thank you, THANK you!" She hung up and began spinning about in circles. "It's Will. The Coast Guard's bringing him home. And Bart Simes, too, for some reason. Oh! Oh!" She stopped her whirling but the room did not. It went faster and faster until she spun in the opposite direction.

"Perhaps if I call your house this instant, I can catch your folks," said Mary Pete, jiggling the receiver for the operator.

Lettie's father answered the call and Mary Pete gave him the joyful news. "No, no, of course not," she ended, "you don't need to come at all. We're doing fine."

"If they have any sense," she said, hanging up, "they'll go to bed and get some sleep. As for us, we've got to be on the welcoming committee. If those Coast Guard boats travel the way I hear they do, we'll have to hustle to get to Bart's wharf ahead of them."

In Mary Pete's old car the four rocketed to the dock. Sim heard the thunder of their running feet as they passed the office. He joined them at the end of the wharf.

A distant hum announced the Coast Guard's coming. Soon, with a muted spluttering, the lifeboat drew alongside the float.

"Holy smokin' oakum," Sim called out in his up-and-then-down voice, "Bart, you old crow, you went off in a yacht and you're back in a lifeboat. What's the idea, have to be rescued?"

Will answered, "The Coast Guard didn't get us. We got them."

Sim seized the line that shot out from the boat and the two passengers stepped onto the lobster-car float. They crossed to the ladder. Will with a foot on the first rung exclaimed, "Why, she's still under there!" He pointed to the dark recesses beneath the dock.

"Who?" asked Lettie, leaning out to look.

"Ebbie's skiff," answered Will. "I tied her up there when I went aboard the *Elmira*. I've been wondering all this time if she went adrift."

"It was the oars that did that," said Mary Pete. "One of them was rescued and brought in. It scared us most out of a year's growth to see it."

"Well, there, sir," Ebbie exclaimed. "You tied her up so snug that she hung there stern down when the tide went out. The oars spilled out and off they traveled. We got one, the other's missing. Well, never mind, it weren't much better than half an oar at that."

Will climbed the ladder and Bart followed.

"Glad you got the lobsters off in good shape. I don't see a single crate here, Sim," said Bart.

Sim looked stunned. His face turned as white as a tanned one can. "Say that again, Bart. The lobsters gone?"

"That's right," said Bart. "I noticed coming in that all the crates we had moored off here are gone."

Sim shook his head. He looked completely bewildered.

"Didn't the truck come for them then?" Bart asked.

"No. Maybe I dozed off or something. I must have, come to think of it, or I couldn't have waked up just now, could I? I had the gun on the ready and I must have gone to sleep sitting there."

Then a red truck came careening down the road and drew up by the dock with a splatter of gravel and a whoosh of air brakes. Large letters on its side said, LOBSTERS.

"Golly, Bart, we did the best we could. Everything went wrong with us the way it does sometimes," the driver called from the cab.

"It's still going wrong," Bart answered. "Your lobsters are gone. I'm cleaned out. Hijackers!"

"Hijackers," the driver repeated. "I can believe it. There's been a lot of such works going on all along the coast."

Bart turned to Sim. "Go along home and get some sleep, Sim. Send your dad down to take over for me and I'll go do likewise. Don't be too cut up about this. It's my fault, too. I should have known better than to leave a man's job to a boy while I went gallivanting off."

The boy hung his head, swallowed as if it hurt, then loped off toward home. Bart went to speak to the truck driver.

Mary Pete, Ebbie, and the three cousins filed past Bart on their way to the car.

"Will can fill you in on what we've been doing," Bart said to Mary Pete. "Later on, toward suppertime, I'll be up.

133

There's a couple of things I'd like to thrash out with you, if you don't mind."

Her answer was noncommittal. "Come ahead, Bart. I'll be 'round . . . in the shop most likely after I've caught up on my sleep."

Ebbie advanced on Bart. His eyes sparkled with excitement. "We saw a lobster smack come in last night," he said. "She was a stranger in these parts and she went straight to your wharf. The others saw her. She's the one that did it; must have towed the whole gang of crates off, just as neat's a pin."

The others went on to Mary Pete's car and left Ebbie to his moment of glory.

"Start talking, Will, and don't skip a thing," said Lettie. "We've waited long enough to know what you've been up to."

CHAPTER EIGHTEEN

MRS. TRAFTON POINTS A FINGER

While they ate breakfast, Will told them the story of his cruise on the *Elmira*. Of course, here at the table with Mary Pete and Ebbie present, he didn't give his true reason for going aboard the yawl. That he would tell only to the "Down-with-Black-Bart Society" when they were alone. Now the curiosity to see the fine boat would be his excuse for having been caught in her cabin.

Soon a drowsy peace settled over the table. Mary Pete pushed back her chair. "If I don't move I'll doze right off here like the Dormouse at the Mad Hatter's tea party. Ebbie, will you trot out to the shop and get out that clock sign of ours? Set the hands at 4 P.M. as the time we'll open up. Put the sign in the window and pull the shade behind it. I doubt if there's anyone in the whole county needs a prescription the way we all need sleep."

Ebbie said as he went off, "I'll fix the sign in the window and then I'll lock myself in over there and sleep like a chuck in his hole."

The three cousins hurried upstairs. Will told them of his changed feelings about Bart. They agreed that there were still many mysteries to be cleared up. Lettie and Jo fairly bristled with "Why's." Why had Bart wanted a new bridge for his enterprise with Harry if he hadn't trusted him from the first? And why in the world hadn't Will found this out from Bart?

"You know as well as I do you don't up and ask grown-ups some things. You have to wait until they want to tell you. Then there was the question of what *I* was doing on the *Elmira*. I didn't want him to ask me that." Will's explanation satisfied the others.

"Besides that mystery, there are plenty of strange things to find out about." Lettie held up one hand to count them on her fingers. "There's the green footprint I saw in the attic. There's who switched around the tags on the dried herbs. There's who snitched the old copybook from the kitchen—"

Jo interrupted. "One thing Will missed when he was off and that was goose-grass greens. They're really gruesome."

"They aren't so bad," Lettie said, more in defense of Mary Pete who favored them than the greens themselves.

"I was trying to wake you up," said Jo, "you were slumping."

"Perhaps if Mary Pete had had the old copybook with the rule for cooking them in it she had—" Her words came slowly and then, like a clock running down, they stopped. Her head dropped down upon her pillow.

"Lettie," said Jo, "goose-grass greens are gruesome."

There was no reply from Lettie, except for a sleepy moan.

"Guess this meeting's over," said Will. "We might as well go to sleep, too."

The whole household slept until the shadows lengthened across the fields. Jo woke first when he heard a loud knock at the back door. Half-awake, he went downstairs.

Bart was in the kitchen, standing on the braided rug before the stove. "Mary Pete about?" he asked. "I see she's shut up shop out there."

Then Mary Pete came into the kitchen. One cheek was rosy as if she had slept on it. When she saw Bart, the other flushed to match.

"Bart, I didn't expect to see you here so soon," she said.

"I didn't plan to come this early but I had a row with Mrs. Ivy Trafton herself and I thought I'd better tell you what about before she could do any more damage," Bart said.

"Oh?" said Mary Pete. She made the word a question.

"When I got to the house this morning Mrs. Trafton was lying on her sofa in the kitchen. She was sort of moaning and groaning. She said she was sick, that you had poisoned her."

"Me?" said Mary Pete.

"That's the way she's talking. She says she ordered some kind of dose from you. She took it and got her side-kick there, that Maybelle Merriweather, to drink some, too. Now she claims they both are sick as dogs. I don't know, of course, but I had the feeling she couldn't wait for me to get back so she could tell me about it. What's almost the worst of all is that she's spreading it around by phone. By now the whole place probably thinks you're a Lucretia Borgia or an African witch doctor."

"There are times I'd like to be, times like this," said Mary Pete. She straightened her shoulders defiantly. "Tell me, Bart, what did you say to Ivy Trafton?"

"I told her plenty. I said I'd have no malicious gossips in my house. I told her to pack her traps and go live with Maybelle," Bart answered.

"I'd take my oath the remedy I fixed for her was okay. Of course, with one thing and another, we had a sort of upset day yesterday. Still, I was careful as could be with the prescriptions. Goodness knows, I have to be always." Mary Pete's forehead was furrowed as she recalled the events of the day before.

"Come on over to the shop with me, will you?" Bart asked. "There are lots of things I want to thrash out with you."

Mary Pete hesitated, but not for long. "Ebbie's asleep over there but I tell you what, let's take a walk along the road a bit. I can keep an eye on the shop and look for the spots where the wild geraniums are thickest."

"Same old Mary Pete. Business as usual," said Bart more with admiration than disapproval.

He and Mary Pete went off and Jo hurried upstairs to tell the other two Bart's startling news.

Soon all three, their faces in a triangle at Lettie's window, watched the two former enemies pacing together.

Lettie, whose chin rested on the sill, asked, "What in the world can they be talking about? It's surely serious, whatever it is."

They never knew everything said on the road that day between Bart and Mary Pete. They did soon discover that he had given their cousin something to think over. When she returned to the house she called upstairs.

"Bring all the duds you have that need to be washed. I'm going up to the Laundromat in town right away." Her voice was urgent.

Soon they brought their laundry to the kitchen.

"Be sure you've emptied your pockets of all junk. We don't want to ruin the washing machine with our treasures."

While they obeyed, she said, "I can always think best while I drive alone. I don't know why, but it's so. That's the reason I'm not issuing invitations for you to come along."

The contents of Jo's dungarees thudded onto the table

as he shook the legs. Mary Pete turned out both pockets of Lettie's cotton bathrobe. "Lucky we did this," she observed. "Here's a comb, and what's this, anything important?"

She held out a strip of cardboard. Lettie took the extended piece from her cousin and blushed. Mary Pete had found her piece of the S.O.S. card. She wouldn't hurt Mary Pete's feelings by telling her how she had hated to come here.

"It's nothing really," Lettie said, and thrust the strip into the kitchen fire.

Mary Pete combed her hair at the mirror beside the kitchen shelf. "Lettie," she said, "this morning Ma'am Maker called and asked me to make her some elderberry tea. I presume she hasn't got the word that I'm a poisoner. Anyhow, she hasn't canceled her order. It's not a hard one to make. I think you could easily do it for me. It's a teaspoonful of elderberry flowers and one of peppermint leaves to a cup of water. After they've steeped in the boiling water, they're strained through cheesecloth. I'll run over and rout up Ebbie and get the ingredients out for you."

"I'd like to make it," said Lettie.

While they talked, Jo had been stowing the articles that had tumbled from his dungarees in his shorts' pocket. In they went, a length of caulking cotton, one black lucky stone banded with white, several shells, one piece of something or other. What was it?

While he turned it in his hand, Mary Pete went out. Suddenly Jo shouted, "Whoops, I'd forgotten all about it. Look, you two."

"What's all the excitement for? That's just a piece of broken dish."

"So 'tis," Jo answered, "but it's not just any dish." He told them how he had unearthed the bit in replacing a red-flagged stake.

Lettie studied it with new interest. "Wowie, it does look ancient for sure. All those blue-and-white curlicues and the big blob of yellow. What's more, there are no dishes like it now in the house. We've been here long enough to know that. Say, it might even date back to the Pilgrims."

"Holy mackerel, it sure does look ancient," Will agreed. "Know what we ought to do, Let? You know that friend of Mum's who works in the museum in Boston? He's an expert on pottery and stuff. She says he can tell the age of most any dish. We ought to send this to him."

"We should," said Lettie firmly. "And let's keep it a secret from Mary Pete. Then if it turns out to be a piece of dish from the five-and-ten and not one from Pilgrim days, she won't be disappointed."

"Let's send it off as soon as we can. Every day counts, and the bridge hearing is getting near. Now's the time we need to know whether the Pilgrims traded with the Indians here."

"You two will have to take care of that." Lettie tried not to sound as important as she felt. "I've got to help Mary Pete."

While Will wrote the letter to Mr. White, the museum expert, Jo prepared the precious pottery bit for mailing. He found a box about the right size, lined it with layers of paper towel, and wrapped it up. It took so long that the boys ran most of the way to the post office to get there before it closed.

"Golly Moses," Jo said as they ran, "if only Lettie hadn't had that idea about not disappointing Mary Pete, we could start right in digging for the rest of that dish. And for whatever else might turn up. Girls always make things so complicated."

"Sure do. I can't wait to have a crack at digging, either," said Will.

Mr. Pottle, the old postmaster, was still in the post office when they arrived. "Good things come in small packages. Want to insure this?" he asked, looking over the top of his glasses at the mark on the weighing scales.

"Yup," said Jo. He ignored his back-handed way of asking what they were mailing.

The postmaster's next remark was harder to leave unanswered. "This is one of them lethal doses of Mary Pete's, no doubt," he said.

"Could be," said Jo. He was too angry to say more.

They paid the postage and went home. Halfway they met Ebbie. He carried a glass jar. "Well, sir, you'd never guess who's up to the house. It's Bart, big as life. He brought some lobsters with him. He's staying for supper. Well, I better get going. Old Ma'am Maker will wonder what's keeping her elderberry tea."

Bart's big car was in the yard. Inside the house, Lettie was entertaining Bart as agreeably as if she had never talked about the "blackness" of Bart.

"Hi, Bart," Will greeted him. "Any clues about the lobster hijackers yet?"

"No clues, unless you call the cut end of a line one. I guess Ebbie is right in thinking the thieves came by water. They must have cut that line of mine and towed off the whole gang of crates. Probably as soon as they got off a safe distance they hauled 'em all aboard and then really skedaddled."

Lettie beamed. "Isn't it lucky that Del Snow came in with enough lobsters for our supper? And Bart's eating with us."

The cousins exchanged glances. With Bart staying for supper, there was a hope that questions might get answered without being asked.

CHAPTER NINETEEN

BART CONFESSES

While the lobsters steamed they kept their hunger at bay with potato chips that Mary Pete had brought back from her trip to the laundry.

"Any word about the stolen lobsters, Bart?" Mary Pete asked.

"None. This has sure taught me a lesson, or several, as a matter of fact. First one is, you don't go around the state telling about your having so many lobsters you need a bridge to sell them. Second one is, I'm not cut out for big business," he said.

"Probably you aren't," Mary Pete answered. "Now why don't you tell these young ones what you told me this afternoon?"

"Okay, I will, but first of all, I'll cleave up these lobsters. They look plenty done to me." Bart carried the great kettle to the sink and drained off the liquid. He laid the lobsters on a chopping board and split them lengthwise with a large butcher knife.

Lettie's curiosity triumphed over her hunger. "Don't forget, Bart, you're going to tell us something," she reminded him.

"No, siree," he said, but before he could begin the latch of the back door rattled and Sim's head poked in the crack of the half-open door.

"Say, Mary Pete, don't you ever answer the phone over there to your shop? Coast Guard's been calling Bart down to the office. I told 'em where you were and to try here. They did try a couple, three times. No answer, so up I came. They want you to call 'em back, Bart."

Bart left at once for the shop next door.

"Come on in, Sim. Join us. Have a claw," Mary Pete invited.

"No, thanks. I'll just go straight back. I'm going to stay close as I can till we discover who took the snappers." His head withdrew. The door slammed.

Before long Bart returned. "There's a customer out there for you, Mary Pete," he announced.

Bart followed Mary Pete to the shop.

"Oh, dear, just when we were getting somewhere," said Lettie. She sighed and snipped off her lobster's two feelers. Mary Pete had showed her how to make coral bracelets from these flexible hollow antennae by thrusting the tapered end into the wider end. Lettie made two of these red circles and then helped herself to the feelers on Will's lobster.

"Can you make out what Mary Pete thinks about Bart?" she asked. "It strikes me she's not half so fierce toward him."

"No matter how she feels, I wish they'd hurry back," said Jo.

By the time Bart came in alone Lettie was wearing as many coral bracelets as a mermaid and all five lobsters had lost their feelers.

143

"That was our friend Vint," Bart told them. "He thought we'd like to know what other things they found aboard the *Elmira*."

He sat down and picked up a lobster leg.

"Go on, don't stop," they begged him.

"Vint says he kept on hunting for stuff after we left. He found another compartment, this time under the deck. It was stuffed full, he said. More Dutch stainless steelware, and some fine English china, even a few pieces of English silver, platters and such. This was antique, so my friend Harry was not only smuggling in new stuff but receiving stolen property as well. That's what they say, at least." Bart took a bite of lobster.

"Holy mackerel," said Jo. "Have they caught Harry yet?"

"Not yet, but they're bound to soon. Someone will discover him in his woodshed and flush him out, that is if the poor fellow emerges from Misery Heath," Bart answered.

"Never mind *him*. What about his boat? What's going to happen to the poor old *Elmira*?" Will asked.

"It seems she wasn't stove up at all from being run aground. The Coast Guard took her off and run her to Allenport under her own power. Later, she'll go to the highest bidder—"

Will broke in, "If only they'd put it off until I could get enough money, but I suppose it would take years."

Bart said, "Buck up. Maybe the two of us together could bring the old *Elmira* back to Surprise."

Once more the door latch rattled. Mary Pete came in. "Gracious, my lobster's probably stone cold. Now, Bart, you shoot and tell them all about it."

"I'll go right back to the beginning," Bart said. "Once upon a time Mary Pete and I were the best of friends and the best of enemies. In other words, we were inseparable. My mother died when I was quite young. This place was sort of my second home; I was in and out all the time. Now, Mary Pete wasn't like the other girls 'round. Can't remember that she ever trundled a doll carriage or went scooping along in her mother's high heels. She was more for going on the water summers and coasting winters and such—"

Mary Pete interrupted, "I wish you could have seen Bart's double-runner sled. It was the fastest in town with a gong fastened underneath it that would wake the dead—"

"And when Mary Pete yelled, 'Clear the lullah,' on those long hills toward town you could hear her clear to Eden Island," Bart went on. "Well, to make a long story short, we had what you might call a falling out. She told me not to come here any more and I said this would be the last place I would come. As time went by, I regretted all this but Mary Pete didn't seem to. I tried to be friendly and got snubbed for it every time. I got missing our old ways more and more. Finally I decided to take a drastic step to make her pay attention to me, even if it was only to shoot me. It's a wonder she didn't do just that. It all began when Harry came on the scene. He had this big idea we should build a bridge to Eden and build a lobster pound out there, have a marina and attract tourists for miles around. I went along with his idea. 'Here's the very way to show Mary Pete I'm pretty good,' thought I—."

Bart sighed and popped a bit of lobster into his mouth.

"We got the bridge idea rolling," he continued. "We got signatures enough to make them really interested at Augusta. Engineers started planning our bridge. Then, suddenly, I had the horrors. They decided the best and only site for the bridge was right where this house sits. This I hadn't foreseen, that one end of the bridge would knock out the old Tibbetts house. I would rather have it my own house, I can tell you."

It was plain that Bart was feeling better for this confession. How Mary Pete was feeling the cousins couldn't be sure. Her eyes stayed downcast although the corners of her lips did turn up.

"Suddenly I thought," Bart continued, "they *can't* take the old house. It would be a crime. I decided not to admit this to Mary Pete in hopes she would come and beg me to help her, to get the whole thing called off. She didn't, not Mary Pete. Every day she got more stern and distant, not to say downright fierce."

"She certainly was the day we came and you passed us on the road," said Will.

"I even swallowed my pride one foggy day this week and came up to see Mary Pete. There was no one in the house —Ebbie was in the shop with her—I could hear his fog-horn voice all the way to the kitchen—so there was no chance for a private talk with her. I wanted to tell her I was getting kind of frightened myself at how fast things were moving. To confess, too, that I never intended when we first started planning this bridge to have it destroy the Tib-betts place. Since we couldn't have our talk that day, I decided to go through with showing the bridge plans on the Fourth of July. Maybe, thought I, that will send the lady running to me, begging for help."

"The bridge picture certainly spoiled the whole day for us," said Lettie.

"You can include me in on that," Bart added quickly. "Gorry, did I hate myself all day, every minute! Harry was due in a couple of days. He and I had plans for a little cruise together. I was going to call a halt to the bridge affair but I wasn't going to do it until I found out what he really was up to. I knew that it was something dishonest, and I kind of suspected smuggling. Now we know. Well, the whole business has been a nightmare but all's well that ends well."

Mary Pete spoke up at that. "The point is, Bart, it's not

ended—at least as far as the bridge plans go. They're still rolling and it's going to be harder to stop them than it was to start them, or I miss my guess. I have nightmares every night that the old house is being torn down over my head. So *nothing* is ended."

"Mary Pete, I give you my word from this moment on all my time and energy are going to undoing those bridge plans. The lobster business can go to pot until we succeed," said Bart.

"We'll help," said Jo.

"You bet," said Will.

"We'll have an anti-bridge club," said Lettie.

"As for me, there's not much I can do," said Mary Pete. "Any squawking I might do would be laid at the door of family pride. You know, those Tibbettses always did think they were someone and so on. I can hear them saying it."

"It's up to the rest of us," said Will. "We'll all get names of people against the bridge. Now they know Bart is against it, the job ought to be easier. You see, Bart, we've tried it and didn't get a single solitary name."

"We'll start tomorrow," said Lettie. "I'll try Mrs. Trafton again, even."

Mary Pete put back her head and shouted, "Clear the lullah!" as loudly as in the old days when she and Bart wanted a clear track for his double runner.

"Now that leaves only two things you haven't confessed to, Bart," said Lettie. "One is, did you take the old copybook from the kitchen shelf on the foggy day you came here? The second is, why did you go up attic and switch around the tags on Mary Pete's herbs?"

"Guilty on the first count, lady," Bart answered. "I borrowed the old copybook to reread the bit about the Indians and see if there were any more old writings that might turn up a clue for saving this place. As to the second, 'tweren't me. Not guilty. I haven't been up attic since Mary Pete and I had our big spat."

"Well, then," said Lettie, "I'm glad of that. Whoever it was switched those tags around, that was Mrs. Trafton's poisoner."

For a moment the others looked bewildered. In all the other excitement of this day, they had forgotten that Mrs. Trafton was pointing her finger at Mary Pete and calling her a poisoner.

CHAPTER TWENTY

CLOSING THE GAP

Bart wrote a splendid new petition against having a bridge to the island. Every day he and the three cousins worked at gathering signatures on it. Every evening the "Anti-Bridge Club," as they now called themselves, met in the old Tibbetts kitchen. Here they compared the list of signers on the new petition with those on the old one.

"We're closing the gap," Lettie exulted as she drew a pencil through the name of a person who had today written his signature on the new paper.

It wasn't easy, by any means, to get the village people to make such a switch. "What does Bart think I be, a weathercock swinging 'round in every breeze?" was the sort of answer they usually got. They learned that, if they didn't walk off after this rebuff, the speaker would talk himself around to signing, almost as if he had meant to all the time. "Never did want the bridge in the first place. Just a waste of the taxpayer's money. I got carried away by Bart's salesmanship in the first place, I guess."

Will elected to cover the water front. Whenever a lobster boat came alongside Bart's wharf, Will was waiting there. When the captain's catch had been sold, out would come the petition and a pencil.

"What you want for this business is water-proof ink," said Del as he wrote his name. He wiped his palms briskly against his oiled clothes. "Well, sir, this sure takes a load off my mind. I was afraid Bart was going to run me ragged getting more lobsters for him if he got his bridge and built his fancy lobster pound and all. Things are best as they are. I hope we get rid of this bridge to nowhere."

Del's remarks were more or less typical of those Will heard at the wharf. By the end of the week, what with his good luck at the dock and the hard work of the other three, several sheets of paper were filled with names. There were enough to give Bart courage to call a state senator for an appointment. He telephoned from Mary Pete's shop where Lettie and her cousin were making what Ebbie called a "sarse."

He was grinning as he hung up at the end of the conversation. "The senator sounded in a good mood," he reported. "He'll see me Friday. I'll have all my arguments marshaled, of course. And wouldn't it be the best argument of all if we got every blessed name from the first petition on our new one?"

Lettie's heart sank a bit at these last words. She was delighted at Bart's good news but she had a secret feeling of shame at not calling on Mrs. Trafton. Every day she found a new excuse for not going to see her. Bart's report of the angry packing up at home didn't provide Lettie with more courage.

Now, with this appointment with the senator set, Lettie would *have* to call on the housekeeper. She resolved to go as soon as she strained the brew she was boiling.

She set out with brisk steps. All too quickly she got as far as the post office. Here was a ready excuse to delay a bit since no one had collected today's mail and it might contain a letter from the Boston museum. She went inside but found that no mail had come with a Boston postmark. Could Mr. White have gone on a long vacation? Perhaps the pottery bit would wait on his desk until it was too late to help them.

With lagging steps Lettie went on. Even with her strong secret reason for the visit she had no clear idea of what she would say when she turned in to Bart's path. As she crept along it she could hear Mrs. Trafton's high voice.

"What be we going to do, Thomasina? There's not a single living soul wants your kittens. Gladys says she'll take you along with me but, 'No kittens, Ma, and that's final.' I just hate the thought of it but we will have to drown your kits. Oh, dear."

A plan of attack sprang into Lettie's mind with lightning swiftness. She ran into the kitchen. "Mrs. Trafton," she began at once, omitting any excuses for her bad manners in bursting in, "I will find a home for your kittens, every single one, if you'll do a favor for me!"

Mrs. Trafton had been leaning over a small brass bedstead behind the stove where a cat nursed her kittens. "Lands, you made me jump most out of my skin," she said, straightening up. Her tone was disapproving but not fierce. She was not wearing a dragon expression, either. "You're one of the young ones at Mary Pete's," she added to explain Lettie's behavior.

"Yes," Lettie answered," and if there's anything I like it's kittens."

"There they be, the lot of them. Course they're cuter when they get their eyes open," said Mrs. Trafton.

Lettie leaned down to look at the family. Curled into the

151

curve of the calico mother's body was a mass of fur: black, white, brown, and striped. "There's five of them," said Mrs. Trafton.

Then Lettie remembered her true reason for choosing to call on the "Dragon Lady." She looked down at the woman's feet. How she kept from shouting, "The Green Footprint," she never knew. For there it was, the same narrow, pointed shape!

She kept her eyes on the kittens until her thoughts stopped whirling.

To her surprise Mrs. Trafton made a friendly move, "Got time to sit and eat a cookie?" she asked.

Lettie took the chair indicated. She was even more surprised when the housekeeper continued, "I'll just get my pen out of the desk. I expect the favor you want is to have me sign that paper you folks are carrying 'round everywhere."

She set a canister on the table and took off the top. "Molasses," she said of the cookies inside; "my grandmother's recipe. Help yourself."

Lettie took one. While she munched on the first bite she thought, *Oh, dear, I almost wish she wasn't being so nice. It's going to make it hard to come right out and call her a poisoner.*

The woman wrote her name on the petition and added a flourish. "There now," she said," I'll just give Maybelle Merriweather a ring to tell her to sign, too. She most generally agrees with me on things."

The voice in Lettie's head said, *Yes, I know, even if it's pretending she's been poisoned.*

Lettie couldn't eat the cookie until she had said, "Mrs. Trafton, you did go up into Mary Pete's attic and mix those tags up, didn't you? You wanted to get her into trouble and you have. It's getting so people don't know whether to trust her or not."

Mrs. Trafton's narrow face went stiff, then softened so much that Lettie feared she was going to cry. "Yes, I did. I didn't like the way she was behaving to Bart. Why, she had him so miserable he could scarcely eat a thing. Of course, he's always wanted to marry her from the very first. After her father died, he thought the time had come they could. Then they had a silly spat over which house they'd live in. Mary Pete was a foolish girl not to come here, all this nice dark woodwork, but no, she must have her own place." Mrs. Trafton paused. "Well, it's all water over the dam. Bart, he told me to pack up and go, and so I am. But what made you ask about my going up attic that way?"

Lettie told her the whole story. Perhaps if Mrs. Trafton felt that her affairs here were "water over the dam" she might be merciful toward Mary Pete.

"Mary Pete never did any harm to you, did she?" Lettie began.

"No, only in hurting Bart that way. I wanted to make him think she was bad so he could forget about her. All I thought about was, this will queer Mary Pete if word gets 'round she was being careless and making people sick. Now I'd give a lot not to have acted so."

She really does look penitent, Lettie thought. Then said, "I'll make a bargain with you, Mrs. Trafton. If you telephone the same folks you called and tell them that Mary Pete's medicine hadn't made you sick, I'll keep mum as can be about your going up attic at her house. Now what would be wrong with that?"

"Nothing," said Mrs. Trafton, "nothing."

"It's a bargain then. Okay?" said Lettie. She was so happy that this dreaded visit had turned out well that she bolted toward the door.

"Your paper with the names," reminded Mrs. Trafton. "You'll remember the kittens, won't you?"

"How could I forget them?" Lettie answered, then ran

all the way home. That evening she called on Maybelle Merriweather and found her waiting to write her fancy name with a flourishing hand. Lettie was able to produce her two new signatures at the "Anti-Bridge Club" meeting that night as if they were trump cards.

"Well, I'll be switched," exclaimed Bart when he saw them. "Those two old hold-outs. How'd you ever get *them* to sign?"

"It wasn't hard," she said. "Sometimes you have to understand people to get them to do something for you."

No one remarked upon the secret smile she wore. They were too absorbed in counting with Bart as he added the total of new names.

"Who would have thought we'd do it, but we have!" he exclaimed. "We have the same number of new signers now as there were old."

"You're going to have one more," said Mary Pete. "I didn't sign the old one, remember? I'm going to sign this. Now I must go and make some elderberry tea for Maybelle. She bowled me over by calling up and saying nothing quite agreed with her as much as that did. Perhaps business will pick up," said Mary Pete.

Lettie, she said nothing.

CHAPTER TWENTY-ONE

S.O.S. MEANS SLOW OUR SUMMER

On the day that Bart drove off in his big black car to talk with the state senator, the whole Tibbetts household kept as busy as possible. They didn't want free time in which to think that Bart might not have success. Both Jo and Will went early to work on the skiff. Lettie worked with Mary Pete in the shop. They were making boneset tea. It was an Indian dose that had a most horrible taste but was good for curing a stubborn summer cold.

Through all that day of waiting the red flags on the engineer's stakes across the lawn blew gayly. By sunset the wind went down and left the flags limp. Still Bart was not back.

When it got dark Mary Pete lit the lamp and put it on the kitchen table. With a pack of old limp cards the family gathered around for games of *Pounce*. The cards were even limper by the time Bart's headlights swung a bright arc across the kitchen wall.

They all ran outside. Before Bart could leave the driver's seat they called, "Did he say 'yes,' Bart?" or "How did it go?"

"The senator's a no-bridge man now. He was glad to have an end to the plans. He said his friends have all been kidding him about this bridge to nowhere," said Bart.

The air was full of, "Hurrah's" and "Good, Bart," repeated over and over. Jo was the first to do something to celebrate this victory. He ran to the first red engineer's stake and uprooted it. The headlights of the car shone over the row. Quickly he and Jo and Lettie pulled up the rest.

"Tomorrow," said Will, as they went toward the house, "we'll have a monster bonfire and burn all the stakes. We'll make a big production of it, speeches and all."

"Golly Moses," said Jo," have you stopped to think there's no reason now why we can't start digging in the yard to look for more pottery bits and pieces? We can't disappoint Mary Pete if the piece we sent off to the museum isn't ancient, can we? I mean the old house is safe. The yard is ours and not the engineers'."

"What's all this?" asked Mary Pete. "What mystery is this?"

"Let's go inside. We can tell you all about it while Bart has his supper," said Lettie.

"Gracious," announced Mary Pete, "I do need to sit down. I've lost all my gimp, as Ebbie would say, from pure pleasure."

"I never thought I'd see the day you'd lose your get-up-and-git, Mary Pete," Bart said. He followed her into the house as naturally as if he lived there.

All three cousins were up very early the next morning. Lettie laughed when she found Will in the woodshed looking for a spade to dig in the yard. "Oh, dear, I thought I'd be like the little pig in the story, you know the one that got up an hour ahead of the wolf to get to the fair without being caught," she said.

"There's another wolf out there already and at it hammer and tongs," her brother answered.

They found Jo digging where he had found the original piece of pottery. He had turned back a square of dew-spangled sod and was poring over a shoveful of earth.

"No parts of that dish yet," he announced, "but look." He extended his palm on which lay an earth-encrusted bit. "Looks like a musket ball, doesn't it?"

"Sure does," said Will.

Each took a square of lawn. They lifted a section of sod, jumping on the spade to cut through grass and roots, and set it to one side.

Lettie found the first pottery fragment. It was blue and white with a yellow line. After her success, talk died out and work got their full attention. By breakfast time they had four pieces. They laid them on a piece of white paper to make their colors stand out and went back for more digging.

They even forgot about going for the mail. It was Ebbie who brought it, waving an envelope over his head as he came into the yard.

"Will," he said, "you've got a typewritten letter."

Will was so excited at hearing from the museum that his eager fingers tore both letter and envelope. No one complained. They crowded close and read the letter together.

"Dear Will," the letter said,

"I was glad to find your package waiting on my desk when I came in this morning. I knew the moment I saw your pottery fragment that you really had something. Your find is indeed old enough to be a Pilgrim pot as you so wisely suspected. Most people think of the Pilgrims as eating from nothing but pewter plates and wooden trenchers. As a matter of fact, they did have a few cher-

157

ished pieces of Dutch Delft. How much good it must have done the Pilgrim women to have them! This means that my answer is, Yes, it could be part of Pilgrim pot. Probably the Pilgrim man who carried it off to that far spot for a trading post was scolded for it by his wife.

Keep on with your digging. I'm sure the rest of the pot is there and who knows what else?"

The letter was signed, "Sincerely yours, Ralph G. White."

"Now I know what, 'My cup runneth over' means," said Lettie. "Let's tell Mary Pete about this."

They found their cousin in the shop. When she had read their letter, she flopped down into Ebbie's rocker. "It's almost too much. First, I learn my house is still my own and now this comes to prove that the old stories we'd heard about it are true," she said. "Do you know what occurs to me? It's this—now that we don't need to worry about saving this place, we don't need to tell anyone about this discovery. We won't have to live in a national shrine and have folks traipsing in and peering around. We won't have to shove our private life under the rug, so to speak. Mercy me, it's all so wonderful! Now I'm almost grateful to Bart. If he hadn't started all this bridge commotion, how different things would be. I'd be living alone, just dimly appreciating the house. You young ones wouldn't be here at all."

"That is too terrible to think about," said Lettie.

"Let's stop digging for a bit. We can get our monster bonfire ready," said Will.

"I know where there's a real cache of good dry driftwood," said Jo. "It's just been waiting for our fire."

"What are we waiting for?" said Will.

They all knew what for. They must ask Mary Pete if she

wanted them to stay on with her. If this were not the old Tibbetts house last year perhaps they shouldn't stay longer.

Jo put this feeling into words for them. "Mary Pete, maybe we ought to go back home now and leave you in peace. I mean, after all you only asked us because the house was being torn down."

"When you put it that way, you don't make me sound very full of hospitality." Mary Pete laughed at Jo's solemn expression. "Of course I wouldn't think of your going. Do you want to?"

"When we first came, we would have liked to take the first bus back. I had an S.O.S. card to send home in case we couldn't stand it here. But now—" Words didn't come to express how Lettie felt. She spread her arms in an embrace wide enough to include the whole Tibbetts place and the sea around it.

"Now," said Jo, taking up where Lettie had left off, "now S.O.S. means Slow Our Summer. If only we could. It's whizzing by and we have so much to do."

"I'll say," said Will. "Get the skiff in the water, explore the islands."

"Dig and find all sorts of Indian things," said Jo.

"Learn the herbs and drugs in the shop so someday I can really help Mary Pete and gather plants for her," said Lettie.

Bart's black car whirled into the yard.

"Is it okay to tell Bart about the Pilgrim pot, Mary Pete?" Will asked her urgently as Bart came toward the shop.

"I don't see why not," their cousin answered. "Bart's going to be in on such things from now on. He asked me the day after he and Will came home with the Coast Guard if I could let bygones be bygones and marry him. Of course, even with our differences, that's what we always talked of, getting married when my father didn't need so much care. Now there doesn't seem to be any reason why not. Bart says he's willing to live here instead of at his house."

She looked so very happy that Lettie gave her a tremendous hug.

"We'll go and get the bonfire ready. We've got even more to celebrate now," said Will.

They ran past Bart at the door, grinning to show their approval of the new state of affairs. They didn't look back at the old house until they reached the shore. There it stood on its eminence, gracious and mysterious, as if it were saying, "Some of my secrets you know, but not all, not all. Keep searching until you find them."

"S.O.S.," said Jo. "I don't want it ever to end."

ABOUT THE AUTHOR

Mrs. Molloy's first book for boys and girls was published in 1942. Since then hardly a year has gone by that hasn't seen a new Molloy book published, among them *The Tower Treasure, Three-Part Island,* and *The Secret of the Old Salem Desk,* as well as *The Mystery of the Pilgrim Trading Post.* Each one has been enthusiastically welcomed by young readers.

Mrs. Molloy received her education at Brimmer School in Boston and Mount Holyoke College. She has travelled very extensively both abroad and in the United States. She now has two children and lives at Exeter Academy where her husband is a teacher.